Praise for TRAIN I RIDE
A *Publishers Weekly* Flying Start

"*Train I Ride* brings readers on a literal and metaphorical journey that is heartbreaking, hilarious, and life-affirming. Teeming with complex characters that manage to be funny and serious all at once, this book reminds readers of the humanity that exists in an often unfair world."

—Ami Polonsky, author of *Gracefully Grayson* and *Threads*

"A harrowing, moving, immersive, and ultimately uplifting debut novel."

—*Kirkus Reviews* (starred review)

"An emotionally expansive and deeply affecting story. Heartbreaking and unforgettable."

—*Publishers Weekly* (starred review)

"In his first novel, Mosier offers a cast of well-drawn characters, an unusual setting, and a rewarding reading experience."

—ALA *Booklist* (starred review)

"A tale that will stay with readers long after they reach the final destination. A strong purchase for middle grade collections."

—*School Library Journal*

"Rydr herself is sympathetic, and she's got a believable voice, a mix of vulnerability, edginess, and raw fury at her rotten luck. Readers who like drama, sentiment, and tidy, tearful endings may find this to be the ticket."

—*The Bulletin of the Center for Children's Books*

OTHER BOOKS BY PAUL MOSIER

Echo's Sister

TRAIN I RIDE

PAUL MOSIER

HARPER

An Imprint of HarperCollinsPublishers

Library of Congress Control Number: 2016935895

ISBN 978-0-06-245574-1

Typography by Kate J. Engbring

18 19 20 21 22   CG/BRR   10 9 8 7 6 5 4 3 2 1

❖

First paperback edition, 2018

For Keri, Eleri, and Harmony.
Home is wherever I find you.

TRAIN I RIDE

1

THE TRAIN I ride is sixteen coaches long. It's got a locomotive, which doesn't look like the ones in books or movies, and some coaches where the rich people sleep on beds, and coaches where everyone else sleeps on seats. And it has a dining car and a car with windows all around and on the ceiling where happy people on vacations dream about good things that await them, and girls whose lives have been torn apart sit and stare miserably at the countryside rolling past.

I was living in Palm Springs, California, because Gramma lived there. She was the one who got stuck taking care of me.

Palm Springs is a place in the middle of an empty desert with gigantic mountains above it. It's so hot in the summer I felt like I'd go up in a poof of smoke, and way up in the mountains above it, the snowy peaks would look down at me and laugh. There are mostly old retired people and nothing to do except play bingo and golf.

Gramma lived in what was pretty much the armpit of Palm Springs. Some days I hated it with all my heart.

But in spite of it not being such a wonderful place, and Gramma not being the warmest or the most entertaining person around, I wasn't happy to leave it behind. It was what I knew—for two years, anyway. It was comfortably dreadful. And now I'm rolling away from it because Gramma can't take care of me anymore.

The train station in Palm Springs is by a highway overpass. It isn't so much a train station as a bus stop with train tracks, and there's sand everywhere. I got on early in the morning with my one big suitcase they checked, and my one bag that I carried, and the one smallish box that is surprisingly heavy for its size. The sheriff or deputy or whatever tipped his hat to me and handed me over to Dorothea.

I'm almost thirteen, but I supposedly need to be

2

watched over by people since I'm traveling alone. And watching over me is Dorothea's job. Dorothea works for Amtrak, which is the name of the train. She's as wide as she is short, and I can tell she's a real stickler for the rules. But she's not all bad. She gives me a tour of the train, including where I'll sit next to her in one of the passenger coaches, and the observation lounge upstairs and the bathrooms downstairs.

"Sixteen coaches long," she says, "counting the locomotives and the luggage car and everything else. You're lucky to have a seat on the second level. You'll have the best view."

Dorothea smiles a lot and asks me how I'm doing and if I need anything. I don't think she can really get me anything but she asks anyway, which may or may not be nice. I haven't made up my mind about that.

I have to sit next to her all the way to Los Angeles. I sit at the window and look at everything we pass. We go past a thousand windmills that spin like crazy giants waving their arms, and ugly transmission lines carrying the electricity all the way to Los Angeles. We go through the gap in the big mountains where every day the cool fog from the Pacific Ocean meets the hot air from the desert and fights with it over which direction the wind will blow. Then down into the basin of Los Angeles, where I'd never been, because Gramma couldn't drive anymore and told me it wasn't worth seeing anyway.

She was wrong. I see homeless people living in cardboard boxes along the tracks, sleeping in the morning sun, the noise of the train I ride thundering by. They have beat-up couches and recliner chairs facing the tracks. The graffiti on the walls of the businesses and warehouses alongside is their decoration, but more alive than the copies of paintings people buy at the mall, put in their living rooms, and show their friends when they have parties and serve cheese fondue, like Gramma's neighbors Les and Ray used to make.

Lots of things that are worth seeing aren't happy things. That's how I see it, anyway. Gramma doesn't have to see those things anymore, but I do.

It's still morning when we pull into Union Station in Los Angeles, and I won't be leaving again until evening, on a different train headed east. But I've been stuck in worse places. It's a big, ornate station with architecture like a Spanish church, like the centuries-old mission we visited on a field trip from my school in Palm Springs. The ceiling is high, and the tall doors are open to cool breezes coming in from the gardens in the courtyard. But it's right in the middle of downtown Los Angeles.

It's busy with people waiting for trains to take them up and down the coast, and across the country like where I am going, and people waiting for local commuter trains to take them to work and then home, or shopping or to beaches or whatever.

I watch the people and try to see if there are any movie stars among them. There are some beautiful people who look like they could be movie stars, but I don't know if movie stars would take trains.

I sit for a while in the pretty courtyard, which has short trees with thorns and tall trees with purple flowers of a kind that I never saw in Palm Springs or when I lived with my mom in New Orleans.

I sit out there in the courtyard trying to draw a picture of the wind turbines I saw. All I have to draw on is a napkin. I used to draw sketches in my journal, but I don't look in my journal anymore. I'd rather have real art paper but I don't, so I pick up extra napkins everywhere I go in case I see something I want to draw.

I try to draw but I can't concentrate.

I think of Gramma, and what I've left behind. I think of the first argument we had after I moved in a couple years ago.

"Gramma, The Chevalier is smoking a cigarette." The Chevalier was her disgusting little dog. He was a tiny Chihuahua, looking like a poster from science class that shows what happens to people who smoke. He had an eye patch on one eye and the other was goopy, and he was bald in places where he scratched too much. He was so small she'd fit him in her pocket and take him to bingo night.

"Dogs don't smoke," she said, and coughed through her menthol cigarette. She was sitting in her bathrobe and slippers on a folding chair on the sad little concrete patio.

"But he *is*," I said. And it was true. His habit was as bad as hers. "It's dangling from his disgusting black lips and it's still lit."

"It's probably just a stick."

"No. It says 'Winterfresh.' And there's smoke coming from it."

"Dogs don't smoke," she repeated. She threw her cigarette butt onto the blindingly white gravel of the yard and reached for another. "Who would light it for him?"

"He picks up the butts you throw on the gravel."

She shook her head as she lit up. "Dogs don't smoke. And if they did, I wouldn't allow it in the house. You and your asthma."

"That's why I'm telling you."

"Shut up, girl," she grumbled. "You're imagining things."

The Chevalier came through the screen door, hacking. The cigarette in his mouth had burned out. I watched as he chewed and swallowed the filter. Then he sneered at me, and I knew that it was his house, not mine. I knew I'd always feel like an unwelcome guest.

"I like your shirt." I'm brought back to the present by a hobo, who has sat down beside me on the bench. He's sunburned and dirty with dark, matted hair.

The shirt he's complimented has a drawing of a piece of toast smiling at a jar of jelly, like they're friends. It was almost new when I got it from the Salvation Army store. "Thanks."

"Say, you don't have a million dollars, do you?"

"No." I wonder if he really liked my shirt or if he just said it so I'd give him a million dollars. I'm glad for the compliment, in any case.

"I'm waiting for a train," he says quietly.

"Me too."

Birds chirp and sing. The sun is warm, the shade is cool.

"I'm going to New York and then riding a paddleboat to Amsterdam."

"So am I." I'm not going to Amsterdam and certainly not by paddleboat, but I don't want him to think he's alone with his crazy idea.

"Splash-splash-splash, all the way."

"Yep." I nod.

He looks over his shoulder. "Aliens are wearing the skins of my friends. They look just like my friends but they're not. So I have to go to Amsterdam."

"Me too," I say, but I don't think it's funny anymore. It must be scary to be inside his head.

A security guard appears. "You gotta move along, pal."

"Okay, pal," he says brightly. He looks to me. "I'll meet you in spring on the *Kerkstraat*."

It sounds like a real place. It sounds like a place in Amsterdam with flower boxes and cafés on the sidewalks. I wonder if he's really been to Amsterdam and whether he's really trying to get back. And though he is friendly and polite, wherever he's headed, I hope I don't end up in the same place.

But I don't want to be going where *I'm* headed either.

Inside the station there are big black boards with white letters, like scoreboards, that show the status of trains. I watch the boards all day long to see where the trains are coming in from, and where they are going to, and whether they will be on time. I do this because I'm not allowed to go out and explore Los Angeles.

Dorothea isn't here to watch me. Los Angeles is where she lives, so she gets to go home and play with her dog and sleep. Instead there's an old guy who stands by the velvet rope surrounding the waiting area. He generally is supposed to make sure that homeless people don't try to sleep in the comfy old seats meant just for Amtrak riders. Every ten seconds he points to me and then his eyes to let me know he's watching me. When I want to go to the bathroom or get a breath of fresh air or get something to eat, I have to tell him so he can come along and lurk nearby, watching. But he definitely isn't going to allow me to explore Los Angeles.

It doesn't really matter, 'cause I don't have my skateboard anyway. It got stolen a long time ago.

Instead I explore the Japanese convenience store inside the station. It's called Hey Jimmee! It's pretty cute and has healthy foods and strange snacks from Japan, and bottled water. The aisles are probably wide enough to turn around without knocking snacks off the shelves, but they're not wide enough when everyone inside is carrying suitcases and wearing backpacks.

I squeeze my way to the refrigerated section and find some Yellowberry yogurt that has a cartoon

9

animal with giant eyes on the package. That's what I get on my first visit. I come back again and again throughout the day.

I eat all the time but I'm still skinny. When we learned about tapeworms in school back in Palm Springs I was sure I had them inside me, eating everything I put in my stomach before I could digest it. It made perfect sense. But the school nurse said that it was normal for a girl my age to be hungry all the time because I'm not done growing and I walk a lot of miles.

The people at social services gave me money that they said would last for the two days it takes to get to Chicago, but I eat and eat, and I spend all of it at Hey Jimmee! before we even leave Union Station.

I bring a California roll with avocado and seaweed and rice onto the train, and a can of almonds. But I eat everything as the train pulls away from Los Angeles.

2

THE SKY IS still light as we roll away. The sun is behind us, bathing the hills of Los Angeles in gold.

On the train, out the windows, you see different things than you see on a highway. You see old things, and sad things, and pretty things, and monstrous things piled alongside the tracks. The old parts of downtowns and their vintage movie theaters with names like The Bijou, and piles of railroad ties and concrete blocks and rusted metal buildings, and rusted cars, and rusted people looking back at you from their dusty yards, and dogs without collars walking nowhere.

I feel like one of the wandering dogs, but I'm on a big train rolling by, and they stop and watch me. I raise my hand to say good-bye.

The sun sets as we pass through a gap in the

mountains. I think to myself that it might be my last California sunset, and I wonder if I care. This place never wanted me anyway. It barely tolerated me.

Once it's dark, staring out the window isn't much of a way to pass the time. I look at my SpongeBob watch, but it's been broken for ages. It's just as well, because it's gonna be two days before we get to Chicago.

I stand to look in my bag up in the luggage rack, to see if there's anything in it to provide a distraction. I hear Dorothea behind me.

"What's in that box?"

I turn to face her. "Jewelry," I answer quickly, without thinking. "Just some things my dad has given me for my birthdays and Christmases. He's a movie director and he spends a lot of time in Europe."

"Oh. Has he done any movies I might know?"

"Probably not. He's French so he mainly does movies that aren't in English. And Americans think they're weird. But they win awards over there."

"You must be very proud."

I shrug. "I think he feels bad about being away so he gives me rubies and pearls and emeralds. I don't really wear them but I guess they're kind of valuable so I'm bringing them with me."

"Oh, I see. Well, I'll be sure to keep an eye on the box for you, honey."

"*Merci*," I say. "That's French for thanks."

She smiles and walks down the aisle.

I'm pretty sure she didn't believe me, but it isn't any of her business what's in the box or whether or not I have a father.

The night gets dark, but it doesn't get quiet. A group of five drunk men who got on in Barstow three stops back have been getting drunker and louder, and Dorothea is getting more and more stressed out. She stays by my side, but occasionally stands in the aisle to speak into her walkie-talkie.

I see the men when they pass by on their way to the restroom, faces shiny and crazed and vacant. I see them bouncing off the seats as they careen down the aisle away from us toward the stairs and down to the restroom, and their scary leering faces as they head back to their seats. They smell like alcohol and smoke and no showers. Dorothea says they've probably been boozing it up in Las Vegas for the past few days.

One of them passes by, and we hear thumping and shouting as he falls down the stairs. Dorothea groans and follows after him, talking into her walkie-talkie again. Another Amtrak conductor, a short guy who walks like a penguin, hurries down the aisle toward them.

I wish I had a book. All I have is a really short book

that I've memorized, so it doesn't really help pass the time or distract me from worrisome things like drunk guys making trouble on the train. I've already read the free paper from Los Angeles that I got in Union Station. I'm left to my own thoughts, which tend to take me places I don't want to go.

Suddenly, I hear Dorothea shouting and my heart starts racing. I lean over to Dorothea's seat and look up and down the aisle. People are asleep or minding their own business.

Another conductor runs to the stairs. I try to disappear into my seat.

Back in New Orleans, my mom used to have public embarrassments. One time we were at a diner for breakfast on my ninth birthday. It was one of my favorite places to have a special meal, in an old dining car that used to be part of a train. They had little jukeboxes at every table that played happy music from a long time ago.

We had just ordered. A big stack of pancakes for me, and hash browns. Mom just got toast and coffee. I knew it was because she didn't have enough money for something better, but she pretended she wasn't very hungry. She looked hungry, though. She always did. Skinny, and ghost-faced.

A guy came up to our table. It was a guy I recognized, and my mom acted surprised to see him. He was always smiling but he was bad news. He was like the man version of her, scrawny and hollow. They talked for a minute while I looked out the window at the rain. Then he left.

My mom said she had to go to the bathroom.

I could tell by her cheery tone that everything was going to get very bad.

She gave me a quarter for the jukebox, and I watched her walk away.

I looked at the songs. I chose "Do It Again" by the Beach Boys 'cause it's the happiest and the furthest away, like a vacation I'll never get to take. I chose "Blue Bayou" by Roy Orbison because it's the saddest.

The food came. The waitress gave me a sympathetic smile, and I hated her for it. I spread the butter on the pancakes and put on as much maple syrup as I wanted. If my mom was at the table, she would have told me to use molasses instead of maple syrup 'cause she said it has more minerals. But she wasn't at the table so I had the maple syrup. It's sweeter.

I filled up on the food. My mom filled up on whatever.

I was taking my last bite of the hash browns when I heard the sirens, and the paramedics rushed past my table and into the bathroom. I recognized the paramedics and I could tell they recognized me, so they knew who they'd be finding in the bathroom and rescuing from the clutches of death. It wasn't the first time I'd seen them and it wouldn't be the last.

I'm brought back by the shock of a guy plopping down in the seat next to me. He's one of the drunks. He smells like he's peed on himself.

"Whaddya doin'?" he slurs.

I turn away from him. I have experience dealing with people like this. It's best to only answer with your feet, whether it's running or kicking. But I'm not in a great position to do either one.

"Hey, you priddy thing, I'm-a talkin' t'yoo."

"I'm not a *thing.*"

"You don't know how to take a compliment*sss.*" He sprays me with spit.

Dorothea appears and grabs his arm. She pulls him into the aisle while he fights back, and I push him away with my feet. Dorothea shouts for help and the drunk guy uses a very bad word. I close my eyes, which is the last option that you hope you never arrive at. More people come to help, passengers and the Amtrak guy who walks like a penguin. They pull the drunk guy away. Someone suggests they shut him in a bathroom. Finally everything is quiet.

The police come on in a town called Needles and take the drunk people from the train. You're not allowed to bring booze on, and they did plenty of other things that were against the law.

We're there for three hours while they're getting them off the train and taking statements from all the people who were involved and who saw it. Including me.

Dorothea finally returns and sits heavily in the aisle seat. I look over to her but she doesn't look back. She puts her face in her hands.

I wish I could say thank you for saving me from the drunk guy, but I can't. I'm too busy being mad at myself for needing to be saved. Needing to be saved is a dangerous spot to find myself in. So I pull the window curtain closed and lean against it, eyes shut. In a while the train starts moving again, and I drift into sleep.

I dream of laundry machines tumbling clothes all night. We never had our own laundry machines in New Orleans, so Mom would take me to the Laundromat.

I'd read books from the library and Mom would bite her nails and watch the people under the fluorescent lights.

I used to like to hide behind the dryers where the air was warm and lavender-scented. I'd sit back there and read and nobody could see me. I was only six and seven years old, so I could fit behind them easily. Then one time I saw a rat back there and I screamed and banged my head on the machine as I got out quick. I never sat back there again.

I WAKE UP with a sore neck, early light soaking through the window. The train makes a tumbling noise like the laundry machines in my dream, but there's no lavender smell, and it's cold from the air-conditioning.

I go to the dining car. It's filled with tables covered with white tablecloths and nice silverware and glasses. The smell of food cooking makes me ache with hunger.

A woman in an Amtrak uniform comes toward me, smiling. "Good morning! What time is your reservation for?" She holds menus against her chest.

"Reservation?"

"Yes, you need a reservation for the dining car. But if you can't wait that long there's a snack bar downstairs from the observation lounge."

"Oh. Okay."

I walk back into the observation lounge and take the stairs down to the snack counter. The food smell here isn't as appetizing, but I don't care.

"Good morning."

I look to the voice and see a guy wearing the train uniform, a long-sleeve white shirt with a black vest and conductor's cap. He's ridiculously good-looking. He has a cleft chin and everything.

"Hey." I look away and back to the snacks. The veggie burger wrapped in plastic looks good. So do the doughnut holes.

"Let me know if you have any questions," he says.

I nod, and walk out and go back up to the observation lounge. I sit at a table and look out the window.

We're moving so slow, and I have so far to go.

"Mind if I join you?"

It's a man with a neatly trimmed gray beard. I shake my head. He sits across the table from me. He's got a cardboard tray with a steaming cup of coffee and a container of doughnut holes.

The coffee smells good. Gramma always made coffee and I got into the habit of drinking it when I stayed with her. I look away.

I hear him peel the wrapper off the container of doughnut holes as I watch some cows get left behind in the morning light. Then I smell them. Cinnamon. He opens a journal of some sort, and I hear his pencil marking the page. I see stacks of railroad ties piled up alongside the tracks.

I hear my stomach growl. So does he.

"Did you say something?" he asks, looking up.

"How are those?" I ask.

"They're not bad. Wanna try one?"

"No thanks."

"Here," he says, and drops one on a napkin in front of me. I stare at it before putting it in my mouth, and the taste almost makes me cry. But I never cry.

"You're right. That's pretty good," I say. "Thanks."

"My pleasure," he says. "Your name is Rider?"

"What?"

"Rider? Is that your name?"

He gestures to the lanyard around my neck. It has a picture of me, and my last name after the word *rider*. It's how the train people keep track of who I am and how I need to be watched by their crew.

"Yep," I lie. I think about how it sounds, my new name.

"That's a cool name."

"Thanks."

"Are your parents hippies?"

"Huh?"

21

"You know, living in a van, wearing bell-bottom jeans, saying everything is 'groovy'?"

"I know what a hippie is."

"Flowers in their hair, traveling the land in search of truth?"

"I *get* it."

"With the name *Rider* I was just guessing they'd be hippies. Which is a good thing, in my opinion." He smiles. He has good teeth, straight and white.

I don't mean to not answer his question. He was nice enough to give me a doughnut hole. But I can't answer. So I just smile, and he goes back to his journal.

He probably thinks I'm a nonconversational kid. Or that I don't really know what a hippie is.

"I'm gonna go down and get some of those," I say. "Can you save my spot at the table?"

"Sure thing," he says.

I breathe into my hand and smell it as I descend the stairs. My breath smells like cinnamon doughnut for the moment. There are a couple of people in the snack area, and I go in and revisit the doughnut holes. There are also candy bars, which sound good even for breakfast, and orange juice and bagels wrapped in plastic. I can smell the coffee.

"Back again," the snack bar guy says. I don't turn around. "What do you like to eat?"

"Everything. Except meat."

"That veggie burger sounds better than it is," he says. "But if you drown it in mayonnaise, you can get through it."

It sounds better to me than he probably intends. I turn around.

"I have a question." My heart is pounding, and I don't know whether it's because I'm embarrassed or something else. "When you have a train ticket do you also have to pay for the food?"

He smiles sympathetically. Just what I was afraid of.

"That's a good question. Yes, sadly, there is an additional charge for the food, which becomes even sadder after you taste it."

"I had a doughnut hole and it was good."

He leans on the counter. "The doughnut holes are the pinnacle of our culinary experience here at the snack counter. The food in the dining car is better. Maybe your parents will take you in there sometime." He says it, and then notices the lanyard around my neck. "Oh, you're traveling alone."

"Yeah, I'm headed to Disneyland to meet up with all my cousins for this big vacation thing."

He smiles. "Sounds like a blast. What's your name?"

"Rider," I say without hesitation.

"You're funny," he says. "I'm Neal." He holds out

his hand. I wipe my hand on my jeans and shake his. I hadn't noticed at any point in my life prior to this exactly how sweaty and pathetic my hand is.

"Hi, Neal."

I get back to my seat in the coach and Dorothea isn't there. She has other duties to attend to, like cleaning bathrooms, which I don't envy her for. As I sit and look out the window it occurs to me I told Neal that I was headed to Disneyland, which is the opposite direction the train is traveling. Plus it makes me sound like such a kid to be going to an amusement park, though he probably noticed that while he isn't old enough to be my father, he is old enough to be a youngish uncle. And he probably has noticed that I am still, in terms of the calendar and the law if not every other single aspect, a kid.

Then I think he may have missed the hole in my story about going to Disneyland. After all, if he's going back and forth constantly for his job, he might lose track of which direction the train is headed at any given moment.

Also, while working for the train he very likely understands that every unaccompanied minor wears a lanyard that has their picture and the word *rider* followed by their last name. But it would only be a matter of time before one of these unaccompanied minors was actually named Rider, and it might as well be me.

It occurs to me that I'm allowing myself to think of Neal being my father. This is just the sort of thing that Dr. Lola, the school psychologist back in Palm Springs, talked about. But it's never happened before. I never saw a man that could make me wish he was the guy coming home every evening. Handsome and always nice, giving me hugs and holding my hand when we'd go walking together. I never had anything like that—ever.

Dr. Lola told me it was dangerous to have that fantasy because some men old enough to be my father might have other terrible plans for me. Neal isn't really old enough to be my father, and he doesn't seem like the kind of guy who would hurt me or anyone else, but I'm still mad at myself for being weak, for being someone who can be hurt.

I think about these things, and his smile and his brown eyes and his warm voice as I nervously stuff doughnut holes into my mouth, which I accidentally stole from Neal and Amtrak. Apparently my hungry hands were looking out for my stomach while the rest of me was hypnotized by his charm. Then I think about the accidentally stolen doughnut holes, and how doughnut holes come and go to the point that gorgeous snack counter attendants probably completely lose track of them. I think of this and wonder if I can ever go back to the snack counter again.

Clearly I am going to need more money if I don't want to starve to death on this train.

I wish I had my invisible monkey with me. He was the best money-making scheme I've ever dreamed up.

In Palm Springs there was a mall where Gramma would take me to get underwear, the one thing I wore that wasn't from the Salvation Army. Every time I went to the mall there was an old man who had a monkey on a leash. The old man and the monkey both wore long-sleeve pink shirts with vertical black stripes, bright green pants, and a porkpie hat. I'm not sure why it's called a porkpie hat, but it's the type of hat old men wear, especially old men with monkey sidekicks.

The old man kept the monkey on a leash like he was afraid he'd run away with the money. Because the monkey, whose name was Jingles, would take a nickel from you, or anything bigger than a nickel, and put it in a little pouch. But Jingles refused pennies. If you tried to give him a penny he'd give you a dirty look and hand it back.

And that was the whole act. You'd give Jingles

money, and he'd keep it. But for five cents you'd get to hand a monkey a nickel, and maybe feel his leathery little fingers touch your palm. It seemed like a pretty good racket, when I thought about it.

When I was ten, I thought it would be great to get into the monkey business. Unfortunately, I didn't have a monkey. But I wasn't going to let that stop me.

One Saturday morning I put on a crazy outfit with socks that didn't match, one leg of my jeans rolled up, and my button-up shirt on backward, which was tricky to do without asking for help from Gramma.

I made a big sign out of poster board and marker that said *Invisible Monkey Shakes Hand For Free. Tips Accepted*. Then I made a small sign that said *Monkey College Fund* and put it on an empty coffee can.

I rode my skateboard to the mall, bringing the stuff with me, and found a planter near the hot-dog place to lean my sign against.

At first people didn't notice me, and they didn't notice my invisible monkey, either. So after scaring up my courage I said in a big voice, "Have you ever seen an invisible monkey? Well, neither have I."

That got a man and woman to stop and smile.

"What's the invisible monkey doing right now?" the man asked.

"He's actually taking a break at the moment, but if

you come back in five minutes you won't be able to see him then."

They laughed. I was pretty pleased with myself, especially after they put a whole paper dollar into my can. Jingles has to work for an hour to get that much money, I bet.

The woman who worked at the sunglasses cart came up and put a dollar in my can. She smiled at me. "Do I just put my hand out and he shakes it?"

My answer came quickly. "He doesn't shake *your* hand. He shakes *his* hand. He's shaking it right now, in fact."

A few people laughed. A small crowd was gathering.

I couldn't believe how well it was going. The dollars kept coming, and so did the jokes. People were gathered in a semicircle around me and my invisible monkey. We made a pretty great team.

"What's the toughest thing about having an invisible monkey for a pet?" someone asked.

"I have to take his word for it that he's brushed his teeth."

The crowd laughed and another woman approached to put a dollar in my can.

Then the old man in the striped shirt and porkpie hat burst through the semicircle, holding Jingles, who looked furious.

"What do you think you're doing?" the old man shouted. "This mall is only big enough for one monkey!"

I couldn't think of anything to say, but someone from the crowd did.

"Come on, old man, she's not hurting anyone."

"Not hurting anyone? I'll tell you who she's hurting! Unlike her *invisible* monkey, my monkey costs real money to feed! And so do I!"

The old man had always seemed so sweet. It broke my heart to see him upset.

He made shooing motions to an empty space in front of his knees.

"Get out of here, invisible monkey! Beat it!"

A couple of people laughed, and a few more objected.

Then the old man put his hand to his head like he was dizzy. Someone helped him sit down on the planter. Jingles screeched.

I grabbed my skateboard and ran. I left behind my sign, my invisible monkey, and the can with all the money in it.

That was the end of my invisible monkey. I never saw the old man or Jingles again, either. I was worried they wouldn't be able to eat after that, and afraid it was my fault.

4

IT'S STILL MORNING when we arrive in
Williams Junction, Arizona. It's been more than
twenty-four hours since I got on the first train in
Palm Springs, but I have a long way to go.

Some passengers get off the train to get on a bus
to take them to another train that will take them to
the Grand Canyon. I guess some people have enough
time on their hands and little enough to care about
that they can take a train just to look at a hole in the
ground.

A nosy old woman with knitting needles has been
trying to make conversation with me at a table in the
observation lounge while I try not to think about food.

"Would you like a cookie, dear? It isn't exactly
breakfast food, but I won't tell."

"No thank you."

Immediately I regret saying no. Being hungry is making me feel hopeless and edgy.

It's also giving me strange thoughts. I think about how the train is moving two thousand miles or whatever down the track, and while it moves down the track people move back and forth, up and down the aisle that runs through the middle of the train and above the tracks. The same aisle that cuts through the passenger coaches also goes through the observation lounge, where there are tables and side-facing seats on either side, and on into the dining car, where the tables are fancier. The same aisle probably goes on through the sleeper cars, but coach passengers aren't allowed to go up there.

So while I can move back and forth on this short line that is the train, the train is on a long line that's pointed toward Chicago, to some new life that everyone seems to think is best for me. But nobody ever asked me how I felt about it.

I look at my SpongeBob watch, which is still broken. We were supposed to be in Flagstaff, Arizona, around sunrise, but the fiasco with the drunk guys has set us way back.

"Are you eager to get where you're going?" the old lady asks.

I shake my head. "I just don't like being late." In reality I'm thinking how there'll be food for me in Chicago. But it's so far away.

"Like I said, try not to think about time when you're riding on a train," Dorothea reminds me as she walks past.

"Crumbling infrastructure," says the guy with the gray beard who shared his doughnut holes with me. "That'll slow us down at some point too." His name is Carlos, which I learn when he introduces himself to the old lady with the knitting needles. Her name is Dot. She talks a lot for a woman with such a short name. And she does it without saying much of anything. We're all sitting together at the same table. Apparently everyone is all chummy on trains.

"What does 'crumbling infrastructure' mean?" I ask.

Carlos smiles. "That means everything is falling apart."

I furrow my brow.

"Don't make the girl sad, Carlos," Dot says.

"He's right." I look out the window at Arizona. Everything here looks crazy, like it was drawn by Dr. Seuss. The plants and rocks, especially in the desert, look like they're from beneath the sea. They look like they were drawn to be silly.

"Where are you headed, Dot?" Carlos asks.

"Kansas City, to visit my sister. I'm looking forward to exchanging some recipes with her and trying them out. Last time we saw each other she had this recipe for mayonnaise cake that sounded just terrible, but it was surprisingly good. I think part of the reason it sounded terrible is because I usually have a jar of salad dressing in the refrigerator instead of actual mayonnaise. And of course salad dressing wouldn't make for a very nice cake, would it? She also had a Nilla wafer pudding surprise that was heavenly. I may just let her do all the cooking this time! Of course her rheumatism is acting up a bit. I should probably at least lend a hand."

I look at Carlos and he gives me a secret smile before he asks Dot, "Why do you take the train?"

People ask this question a lot on the train. What they mean is, *Are you afraid of flying?* But nobody ever asks it that way. I'm afraid Dot will give another long-winded answer so I make my eyes big at Carlos to scold him for asking her a question.

She smiles and looks out the window. "I like the scenery, the slow pace. I like meeting people. I've learned that I'm not in any hurry to get anywhere, so I just try to enjoy the ride."

"I'm not afraid of flying," I say. They both look at me and smile, like they have me figured out.

My stomach growls. I should have said yes to the cookie. Dr. Lola said I have a hard time trusting women. But I trusted Dr. Lola. She was the only woman who never tried to find a way out of taking care of me.

"I'm a professional magician," I say.

"Really?" Carlos asks.

"Yeah. I do birthdays and bat mitzvahs and stuff. Do you wanna see a trick?"

"Sure."

"It costs a dollar. And I need a paper dollar to perform the trick."

Carlos leans to the side to take the wallet from his back pocket. He gives me a crisp five.

"Do you have two paper clips?"

Carlos raises his eyebrows, but Dot starts fishing in her purse.

"I probably do, dear. Oh, how did that get in there? Anyone want an old stick of gum?"

I nod. She hands it to me and keeps searching. I chew the sad-tasting gum as she drops a handful of debris from the bottom of her purse onto the table. There's an aspirin and a thimble and some pennies and nickels and dimes, and a raffle ticket, and a safety pin and three paper clips. She picks up the raffle ticket and looks at it.

"May I?" I ask, my fingers poised above the paper clips.

"Of course."

"So, in this amazing trick I will fold the bill into three panels in the shape of the letter *Z*. Then I put the two paper clips onto it. The first paper clip connects the first and second panels, and the second paper clip connects the second and third, like so." Carlos smiles, amused. "The trick is, I'll pull the ends of the five-dollar bill apart, and the two paper clips will be magically joined, and the bill will remain intact."

"What if it doesn't work?" Dot asks.

"Then the paper clips remain apart and the bill is shredded."

"Do I get the five back if you shred it?" Carlos asks.

"I never shred. I'm magical. Okay, now don't blink or you'll miss it. I'm going to close my eyes and call upon the powers of the magicians who have passed to the other side to assist me."

"Dead magicians?" Dot asks. She pretends to be creeped out.

I smile. "I also close my eyes because the paper clips tend to jump up into my face. Okay. One, two, *three*."

There's supposed to be the snap of the paper like when you shake out laundry, and the ting of the paper clips coming together. Instead there's the rip of the five-dollar bill and the weak clinks of two paper clips falling to the table. Then the sound of Carlos laughing.

"*Carlos,*" Dot reprimands him.

I drop the two torn halves of the five on the table. "Excuse me," I say, and get up from the table.

I think I was thrown off by the fact that it was a five and not a one. I can't afford to have my tricks not work. Where I'm going, I'll need every trick in the book.

I walk down the aisle and through one of the gaps into the next car. To leave one car, you push on a panel and the door slides open, and then you walk two or three steps, push another panel, and a door slides open to the next car. In between it's noisier and harder to walk.

I go down the next stairway to the lower level and into one of the bathrooms. They're tiny, and smelly. They're getting smellier as the trip wears on.

I wash my hands and look at myself in the mirror. I look like I haven't slept for my whole life. Aside from that, I have green eyes and some freckles. I look bored. I look bored even though my hair is dyed bright green like candy. Gramma would have never allowed me to dye my hair green or give myself punk-rock haircuts, but she was nearly blind and kept her house dark, so she never knew.

Grown-ups always say, *You're so pretty, why don't*

you smile? You'd be so beautiful if you'd just be happy. Gramma never told me to smile. I don't know whether she thought I was pretty, but she knew too much to ask me to be happy. She didn't think people should expect to be happy, and she certainly didn't think I deserved to be.

Sometimes I feel like making myself ugly on the outside to match the way I feel on the inside. Then maybe people would stop asking me to smile.

I think about trying to pee but I look at the disgusting toilet and decide not to. I wash my hands again and leave the bathroom.

I pass by my seat and check on my bag and the heavy little black box to make sure they're still there. I don't know where they would go or who would possibly want them, but I check anyway. Then I go back to the observation car, nod at Carlos and Dot, and go down the stairs.

"Hello, Rider," Neal says.

I look up at him like I wasn't expecting to see him. "Hi. I'm sorry, what was your name again?"

"Neal." He smiles.

"Neal," I repeat. "Hi, Neal. I'll try to remember it." His name has been stuck in my head ever since I saw him, but there's no way I'm gonna let him know that.

"Are you hungry yet?" he asks.

"Well, I just had a humongous breakfast in the dining car."

"Ah. You like?"

I run my fingertips over the snack selection. "It was okay."

"I like your hair," he says.

I touch it, moving it behind my ear. "Thanks."

"When I was about your age I dyed my hair blue."

I turn to him and feel myself smiling. "Really?"

"Yep. It didn't turn out as well as yours."

"You have to take the color out first. And then put it back in."

He rings up someone buying an orange. "I think I did it 'cause I was mad at my parents," he says.

I turn away from him and look at the fruit. I pick up three oranges and start juggling them. I learned how to do that when I was, like, seven.

"Nice," he says.

When I hear his voice they fall to the floor. They try to roll away with the movement of the train as I try to pick them up.

"I'm out of practice," I say.

"You can keep those. Work on your act to pass the time."

"Really? Thanks."

"No, thank *you*. For keeping me entertained."

I bring one of the oranges to my nose and smell it. I feel my heart beating. "Well, I better go practice."

He tips his cap to me. "Come back and visit soon. Your face makes me happy."

I smile, but my eyes feel melty, so I turn away and run up the stairs, almost knocking over an old man coming down.

Sometimes I just need an impossible wish to convince me to take another breath, another step. Right now my impossible wish is that I have a dad and his name is Neal.

Back at my seat I'm glad that Dorothea isn't there to see me eating. My fingers tremble as I tear open the oranges. They're sweet, and juicy, and they were given to me by a beautiful saint.

When I finish eating them I smell my hands. They smell like an instant replay of the happiness I've just felt. I put the peels into the pocket of my hoodie and sit looking out the window, hands cupped over my mouth and nose, breathing it in, holding it inside me, and letting it out.

I drift off to sleep and dream of oranges, and of Gramma, whose trailer sometimes had the smell of orange blossoms coming in the window. I dream I'm in Palm Springs, riding my skateboard. It's dusk in winter, and the light is disappearing quickly. I hear Gramma calling my name, but when I rush home to the trailer she isn't there. She's nowhere to be found, and everything is in cardboard boxes. The smell of cigarettes is gone, replaced with the fragrance of orange blossoms.

I wake up and look at my SpongeBob watch, but it's still broken.

We're in Flagstaff, Arizona, and new faces get on the train.

I'm hungry again.

Gramma used to fix the best pancakes. She had a cast-iron skillet, and she'd melt a bit of butter on it as it warmed while she cracked the eggs and mixed the batter. Then she'd pour it on the skillet and I'd watch the bubbles appear until it was time to flip them over. I'd offer to help but she said she'd do it until they put her in the ground, and when they put her in the ground I'd know how to do it from watching her.

One morning in late spring, after the orange blossoms had fallen from the tree outside the kitchen window of Gramma's trailer, I stood watching her make pancakes for my breakfast. She poured the batter in the iron skillet. The batter hissed; the fragrant steam rose to my nostrils.

"You can take it from here," she said. "I ain't feelin' well."

She put the spatula down and shuffled off to her bedroom.

I picked up the spatula and watched the batter. I had seen her do it so many times. The bubbles appeared at the edges but I waited until they spread to the middle of the pancake. I knew that once the pancake loses contact with the griddle, it can never have the right contact again, so I waited an extra ten seconds to be sure. Then I slid the spatula beneath it, lifted, and flipped with a swift, fearless motion.

The cooked side facing me was golden brown, and the batter side made just the right contact with the hot iron.

Perfect.

With the second side there are no bubbles to watch for on top, so I waited until the middle no longer looked gooey, and the pancake had risen from the skillet. Then I lifted it onto a plate and poured in the batter for another, after melting a fresh tab of butter on the griddle. That was Gramma's secret for making it taste the best—using butter instead of oil.

When they were done I sat down at the table with a glass of cold milk. They were warm, cooked through evenly, with just the right amount of butter and maple syrup. They tasted amazing. I wondered whether I should tell Gramma how good they were. I decided I'd better downplay it so she wouldn't think I was being sassy.

Finished, I washed the plate and fork by hand and put them in the rack to dry.

The trailer was quiet. Through the glass door I could see The Chevalier, sleeping in the sun.

I walked to her bedroom and stood in the doorway.

"Gramma?"

My shoulders sagged. I approached the bed slowly, and got down on my knees beside it. Her eyes were wide and unseeing, her mouth agape. I watched the fabric of her *God Bless America* nightgown for a moment to see if she was breathing, but she was absolutely still.

I closed my eyes and dropped back until I sat on my heels. I took a deep breath, held it, and let it out. I did this for a while, until I felt ready to face all of it.

First I shut her eyes and mouth, then combed her hair away from her face, freeing the tangles until the gray almost shined. With a wet washcloth I wiped the corners of her mouth, wiped away the scowl.

Then I covered her dirty old feet with a quilt, arranged her lifeless hands across her chest, and kissed her temple.

She wasn't my mother. She was a grumpy old lady who bought me underwear, taught me how to make pancakes, kept me alive. She wasn't my mother, but I did for her dead body what I wished I could have done for my mom's, instead of just running away.

I filled The Chevalier's water bowl and walked next door to Les and Ray's. They held me, they called 911, they went with me to get my things from Gramma's trailer, but in the end they had to let me go.

I sigh, and look from the back of the seat in front of me to the view of pine trees outside the window, to wash away the memory.

I wonder if there'll be a skillet where I'm headed. I wonder if there'll be everything I need to make the batter.

Done with helping the new passengers board, Dorothea comes to check on me.

"How you feelin', honey?" she asks.

"Just fine," I say. When I talk to Dorothea I can feel my heritage slipping out. My mom was born in South Carolina, and we lived in New Orleans, and sometimes she'd talk that way, all twangy and polite. Especially when she needed something from someone. And sometimes when I'm talking to people from the South, I'll hear it in my own voice. It kind of faded away the couple of years I was in Palm Springs, but it comes back easily.

Now, riding the train, I don't know where exactly I belong.

"Albuquerque is the next stop where you can get off and stretch your legs," Dorothea says. "It'll be a while, but if you're awake and you'd like to get some fresh air, let me know and we can get off together, okay?"

"Okay," I say.

She smiles, and heads off to do her job.

Flagstaff looks nice. It's in the forest, and there are big mountains towering above, with snow at the top, even now in June. Some of the people who get on look like they've been hiking, and they smell like it too. Like sweat and campfire.

Which reminds me. I stand up and grab my carry-on bag from the rack above my seat. Inside is a deodorant stick. It smells like lavender, like the Laundromat in New Orleans. I look up and down the aisle to make sure nobody is coming, and then reach under my shirt to apply it.

Putting the deodorant back, I see my journal. I ignore it, and stow the bag on the rack next to the black box.

I sit down again and look out the window. We've left town now and are in the woods.

If I were writing in my journal I would tell it about everything that has happened, and the people I have met on the train. I don't want to do that right now. I don't want to see the words my mom wrote on the first page, or see everything I've written in it flash past my eyes, especially the last words I wrote. So I leave it up there in the bag she gave me, the bag with the flowers and hearts.

I jump from my seat and rush down the aisle, through the coach and into the observation car. It's filled with the new faces, people playing cards, and I head downstairs to the snack counter. When I arrive I see a sign hanging on a velvet rope that tells me the snack counter is closed.

I turn around. There's a sunburned man with blond dreadlocks sleeping on the floor next to a backpack.

I rush back up the stairs from the observation lounge, down the aisle into my coach. I see Dorothea talking to a passenger. I can hear my breathing.

"Hey, honey, are you okay?"

"Yes."

"Do you need your puffer?"

I hate it when people call it a puffer. I shake my head.

"Are you hungry?"

"No, I—yes."

Dorothea smiles, like she's got me figured out again. "Neal is taking a break, but he'll be back in there in about a half hour."

"Okay. Thanks." I feel relief, and then realize I was worried Neal wasn't on the train anymore. The crew changes every now and then and I was afraid he'd gotten off in Flagstaff.

"But if you're hungry I might be able to find something for you before then."

"No. I mean, yes. Please. Thank you."

"No problem. Have a seat and I'll be just a sec."

I find my seat and sit, feeling better. I try not to feel, mostly. I've gotten good at distracting myself. Ever since I spent the money social services gave me on snacks at Union Station in Los Angeles before I got on the train, I've found that feeling incredibly hungry is a good way to not feel anything else. But feeling incredibly hungry isn't much of an alternative, so I'd rather return to distracting myself in the other ways I've learned.

One of these is my favorite book, and I take it from my bag. It's really not much of a read, and it's too short and familiar to make the time pass on this train. Maybe it's more like a security blanket in the shape of a book. It's called *The Sun Is Shining*, and it's incredibly sappy. But it works. I know it practically by heart, but I open it and begin reading. It's almost a chant.

The sun is shining, and shining are the stars.
The sun shines near, the stars shine far.
Bright is my spirit, bright are my eyes.
Illuminate my path, decorate the skies.

It's small enough to fit in a big pocket, and I've carried it around so much that the corners are rounded. Sometimes it feels like a lullaby, and sometimes it feels like a big lie that I want to believe.

I have it memorized so I don't even need to read it. But I like the shape of the letters and the way they look on the page.

"Do you like nuts?" Dorothea sits beside me, holding a bag of almonds and walnuts and pecans.

I shut the book and nod. "Thank you." I take it with both hands and pull it open with too much force, and a few of the nuts fly up from the bag and then down to my lap. Dorothea chuckles and leaves.

I fill up on the nuts and *The Sun Is Shining*, believing its lies because I need to. Believing it when I need to let it save me is an agreement I have with myself.

I don't know. Maybe it isn't a lie. Maybe the sun is shining somewhere.

Between Flagstaff and New Mexico, the forest thins out and disappears, and the land becomes a vast stretch of yellow grass with very short cliffs and shallow canyons. The only trees are in places where the water goes when it rains.

The train spends part of the time along the path of old Route 66, and I see some of the architecture from the early days of highways that it's famous for, like a motel made of fake teepees. I learn all this from Carlos, back at the table with him in the observation car.

He and I are doing a crossword with Dot, who's also knitting.

"*Working class.* Eleven letters. Starts with a *p*."

I move my lips silently as my fingers count under the table. "Proletariat."

"Where do you learn these words?" The tip of his pencil taps on the spaces. "That works." He writes it in. Dot smiles and shakes her head.

My mom used to read me her old college texts because there was never money for children's books. So I heard *The Communist Manifesto* at an early age. Then there wasn't money for her drug habit so she sold the college texts, and there weren't any books at all.

"Next clue: *beige adventurers.*" Carlos smiles, holding the sharp pencil poised.

Dot cranes her neck and looks at the paper. "What?"

Carlos nods over my shoulder, and I turn to see four

wilderness scouts sitting two tables behind me. My eyes go back to the crossword, but from the quick look I see they're all boys of about my age, wearing beige scout uniforms in various states of disarray. One of them is very cute.

"That isn't really a clue," Carlos says. "I just wanted Rider to understand that there are some insufficiently supervised rogue youth conducting reconnaissance on her."

"What does that mean?" I ask. But I've got a pretty good idea.

"It means they're checking you out, honey," Dot says.

I roll my eyes. "Probably making fun of my hair."

Carlos and Dot look at each other.

"Ah, youth," Carlos says. I know what *ah* means and I know what *youth* means, but I have no idea what he means in saying *Ah, youth*.

We finish the crossword and I head back toward my seat. I push the panel to exit the observation car, and in the vestibule between cars stands one of the scout boys. He has sandy-colored hair swept across his forehead, a crooked smile, and he's holding a small guitar. He's more or less standing in my way.

"Hey," he says.

"*Excuse* me," I say, trying to get past him.

He doesn't budge. "You like playing blackjack?"

"I don't know. I've never played."

"We're having a little game later on. Before 'Taps.' Playing for a little money to make it interesting."

Money does sound interesting. But I don't have any.

"I didn't bring my money," I say.

"That's okay. I can loan you a couple dollars." I flinch as he pushes my hair out of my eyes. "I'll win them back from you anyway."

I scoff. "Where and when?"

"Observation lounge, after sundown. Let's say nine o'clock."

"Don't touch my hair without my permission."

"See you then," he says, and saunters off.

I plow through the next door to my coach. I fall into my seat, exasperated. Then I stand and fetch my hearts-and-flowers bag from the rack, and get out my cherry ChapStick. I put some on and stare at the back of the seat in front of me.

If I want to win some money from him I'll have to figure out how to play blackjack.

I GO BACK through the lounge and down to the snack counter. Neal is back and open for business.

I don't mean to look at the snacks but I do.

"Hello, Rider. What news from above?"

"Hi, Nick," I say.

"It's Neal," he says, smiling.

"Sorry. *Neal.* I'm playing blackjack later and I've never played before, so I was hoping for some pointers."

"Ah, let me guess. If my recollections of childhood are any indication, I'd guess you're playing cards with the boys in beige?"

"Yep."

He shakes his head. "Well, it's not really my thing, but I do know that generally speaking, you'll want to stay when you're at sixteen or greater."

"What does that mean?"

So he explains all he knows about the game, how everyone gets two cards to start, one up and one down, and how you want to get to twenty-one or as close as possible without going over, and how an ace can be worth one or eleven, and how you should stop asking for more cards when you are at sixteen or more. It's confusing, but he writes the important bits on a scrap of register paper.

"Thanks," I say.

"Good luck," he says. "And remember, don't let yourself feel lucky. Just stick to the formula."

"Don't feel lucky. Stick to the formula. Got it."

I sit at my seat looking out the window at the sea of pale yellow grass, thinking about the blackjack rules, wondering whether it's something dads teach to their daughters. If I had a dad maybe I'd have already known how to play blackjack and poker and other card games besides bingo. Bingo is obviously a game grammas teach you.

I'm imagining myself sticking to the formula and beating the scouts at their stupid card game. But my thoughts drift, and soon I'm thinking of a conversation about boys the last time I sat in Dr. Lola's office in Palm Springs. It was the second-to-last week of school, but the very last day for me.

We were in our usual arrangement, with me sitting on the middle cushion of the couch in her dimly lit therapy room, and her across from me in a high-backed chair.

"How do you feel?" she asked. Shrinks mainly try to get you to talk and say things you'd rather not say.

"Amazing," I said.

She didn't smile. "I'm going to miss you."

I folded my arms. "I'm sure there're lots of other crazy kids to keep you company."

"How are you feeling about your grandmother?"

"Where's your yellow pad?" I asked. "How will anyone know we met without your yellow pad?"

She sighed. "I can make notes later. But I'd like to know how you're feeling about—"

"She hated you. She didn't like me seeing you."

Dr. Lola sat up straight and smoothed her skirt. She was pretty, and always composed. "Why do you think that was?"

"She said your name sounded more like a floozy than a doctor."

She smiled. "I've heard that before. But presuming I am an actual psychologist, why do you think she didn't like for you to see me?"

"Because it made her look bad that she had a crazy granddaughter."

"Did she say that?"

I scoffed. "Look at me. I'm not the kind of grand-daughter she could brag about. I'm not an honor student. I'm not good at sports. I'm not beautiful. I'm green-haired and mopey and I don't have any friends."

She leaned forward. "Okay, let's look at those statements one at a time. It's true that you're not an honor student. But why is that?"

"Because I'm not."

"Would you like to be?"

I bit a thumbnail. "I don't know. Maybe."

"Do you think you could be if you worked at it?"

She gave me a moment to respond but I didn't.

"I'll take that as a yes. Now the sports. Do you dream of carrying the team to victory?"

"No. I don't get why people like sports. Or the idea of being on a team."

"I get that. But you're athletic. You ride a skate-board well."

"Until it got stolen. But I only did it to get around."

"And *boxing*."

I raised my eyebrows. "I can't believe you just joked about that. I don't even believe in boxing."

She sat back and crossed her legs. "Of course I can't condone violence. But my distaste for it in that particular instance is mitigated by the odds. There were four of them and one of you. They initiated the hostilities. And I was glad you loved yourself enough to fight back." She smiled. "That's how I described it in your file."

I felt pressure behind my eyes. "Thank you for that."

"Regarding the idea that you're not beautiful, I don't think I've ever met a twelve-year-old who felt beautiful, so I'll give you a free pass on that one. It's true that you're green-haired, but unless I am mistaken, that is not by genetics but rather a choice."

"Correct."

"And a choice made in order to?"

"Get back at my mom. And piss off my gramma. But she didn't see well enough to notice."

"And in spite of how bright your green hair is and how well it sets off your light skin and freckles, I do suppose you are a bit mopey. But you are, after all, twelve, and you've been through more difficult situations than most people my own age."

"That didn't matter to Gramma."

"But does it matter to you? Do you think you can forgive yourself for not having a spring in your step and a song in your heart?"

I fought back a smile. "You're really letting it all hang out on our last day together, aren't you?"

She smiled and leaned forward. "And while you may see yourself as not having any friends, it doesn't mean that you're unworthy as a friend. And speaking for myself, not as a psychologist but as a human being, getting to know you has enriched my life." She took off her glasses and wiped her eyes. "Believe me, that's not something I'd say to every student that passes through my office."

I couldn't think of anything to say to that. Luckily I was saved by the three o'clock bell.

She leaned back and said, "Before you go, let me say one thing about boys."

"Idiots."

"Well, perhaps. But there may come a time in the not-too-distant future when you meet a boy, or any kind of person, whose affection for you, or apparent affection for you, and praise, makes you feel everything you've ever wanted to feel."

"I doubt it."

"Loved, attractive, special, important. *Don't trust that feeling.*"

"It does sound terrible."

She stood and moved toward me. "*Beware* of that feeling. Find it from yourself first. Love yourself." She reached out her hand to pull me up from the couch. "Work at becoming the person you want to be. And love yourself. Only then can you really trust your feelings and the intentions of others."

I couldn't look her in the eyes. And she wouldn't let go of my hand. She put her arm around my shoulders.

"You aren't supposed to hug me." It was true. I read it in the Patient/Doctor Relationship pamphlet.

I pulled myself away, slunk from her office, and left that school forever.

The voice on the speaker says the first wave of people with reservations for lunch are welcome in the dining car. My stomach growls in response.

I'm excited about the prospect of winning money from the scouts later, but that doesn't do me any good right now. I'm starving.

I walk to the observation lounge. Everywhere people are snacking, and the smell of real food drifts in from the dining car.

I want it to look like there was a reason for me to come to the lounge, so I grab a timetable from the display rack. It shows the route of the train and when it gets to different places. I open it up and look at it. Then I grab all of them.

I make my way from the lounge car and into the coaches. I walk down the aisle waiting for courage. A middle-aged woman looks up at me and smiles.

"Would you like a timetable? They're fifty cents."

She looks surprised, then confused. Then she fishes a dollar from her purse.

"I don't have change," I say.

"You can keep it."

I do a little bow. "Thank you, and please let me know if you have any difficulty understanding the timetable."

"Okay."

"For instance, you might need to be reminded that when you are looking at the schedule in one direction you read it top to bottom, and the other direction you read it bottom to top."

"Got it."

"And there are time zone changes. But remember that in Arizona they don't go on daylight savings time."

She's starting to look annoyed, so I walk away, heart racing. I keep moving down the aisle, waiting for eye contact. The next eyes belong to a man with dark hair.

"Hello. Would you care for a timetable? They're fifty cents."

"Que?"

I hold it up. "A timetable."

"Oh."

I notice his accent. He's a Spanish speaker. He

reaches for the timetable.

"*Gracias.* Thank you."

I smile and wait. He doesn't notice I'm still standing there.

"It's fifty cents."

"*Que?*"

"Fifty cents. Please."

"Honey, you can't be borrowin' money from other passengers."

Dorothea has appeared.

"I'm not borrowing it. I'm selling him the timetable . . ." As soon as I say it I realize she'll probably object.

"Honey, you can't take free timetables from Amtrak and sell them to passengers."

"But I'm also offering invaluable assistance interpreting the timetables. Which are a little confusing."

Dorothea stands with her hands on her hips. She doesn't look happy. And she can block your escape with her body if she wants to. She's hard to slip past.

I change directions. "Why does 'invaluable' mean valuable? 'Cause it sounds like it means *not* valuable."

"Honey, you need to give him his money back."

"He didn't give me any yet. I was closing the deal when you showed up."

She says something to him in Spanish. He shakes

his head. She looks back to me.

"Did you take any money from anyone else?"

I hang my head. "Just one."

Dorothea follows me to the woman who bought a timetable and watches while I return the dollar. The woman gives me a faint smile.

Dorothea isn't finished. "Say you're sorry."

"You're not my mother." I feel bad as soon as it comes out. 'Cause she's pretty much all the mother I've got at this point. But she looks sad for me instead of mad at me for saying it. "*Sorry*," I mumble.

My mother would probably have asked me to say I was sorry too. If she had been around.

A little later I am stalking the observation lounge, hungry. It's impossible to make any money with Dorothea now watching my every move, and I'm getting desperate. Walking past one of the tall cardboard garbage boxes I see part of a soft pretzel, sort of resting on top of a paper plate.

My heart speeds up. I go downstairs and get two mustard packs, five mayonnaise packs, and a handful of napkins. Back upstairs I crumple one of the napkins and reach into the garbage to drop it in, then grab the pretzel as my hand exits.

I feel like everyone in the observation lounge is

watching me. It isn't the first time in my life I've done this. When Mom worked at a chicken and waffles place when I was six, sometimes she'd just have me hang around while she worked because she couldn't get a sitter. And I sometimes took food off of people's plates after they left. Even though it was kind of like *used* food, it looked too good to resist.

I hurry back to my seat.

It's less than half of a soft pretzel. There are a lot of different mouths on the train, so I decide to tell myself it was someone with nice clean teeth, like Carlos, who was eating it, but I break off the very end with the teeth marks anyway.

My hands tremble as I squeeze on the mayonnaise and mustard. The pretzel isn't very soft, and the mustard makes me cough 'cause I put too much on.

It's the worst meal of my life. I crowd out the taste with the prayer I was taught in preschool. *God is great, God is good, and we thank him for our food.*

I eat it as quickly as possible so I can begin forgetting it. Maybe my next meal will be better.

I'M BACK SITTING in the observation lounge as the sun gets lower. It's been a full day since this train left Los Angeles, and maybe an hour since the half-eaten soft pretzel. The faint taste of mustard lingers in my mouth, nauseating me.

A man who works for Amtrak as a tour guide is speaking into a microphone, talking about the things we pass, like the dim-witted longhorns. We go through the town of Lamy, New Mexico, which is tiny and looks like the kind of place that Billy the Kid would have hidden in the old days.

The tour guide says that in 1880 the people who lived in Lamy saw a hot-air balloon shaped like a fish float over the town, with the people riding in it laughing and singing and shouting in another language.

Then the people riding in the balloon dropped a rose tied to a letter and a strange cup. The letter was written in characters of some Asian language.

The tour guide keeps talking and moves on to other topics, but I'm stuck thinking about the fish-shaped balloon, wondering if it had floated all the way from China, and wondering where the people on it were going, and what they were laughing about. If I flew on a balloon all the way from China in 1880 and I was looking down on cowboys in a tiny town with dirt roads, I'd probably be laughing too.

I think about what the letter would say. Somebody supposedly bought the letter and the cup and took it away so nobody ever knew what it said, but if they did I imagine it would translate something like

> *Dear people below—*
>
> *We don't mean to be rude laughing at your dusty little town, but we have just flown across the Pacific Ocean in a balloon shaped like a fish. We are eating noodle soup and drinking tea out of cups just like the one attached to this note. Best wishes, and don't forget to wash behind your ears.*
>
> *Sincerely,*
> *Your friends in the flying fish*

I think about how strange it would have been to be traveling all the way from Asia in a balloon shaped like a fish, and I think about how strange it would be to be standing below in Lamy, New Mexico, watching it floating by. I think about writing these thoughts in my journal and then remember I'm not writing in my journal anymore.

Carlos does, though. He's got his journal out, across the table from me.

"What are you writing?"

He looks up. "Journaling, taking notes. I write poems."

"Really?"

He sets his pen down. "Yeah. Do you like poetry?"

"I feel like I don't always understand it."

"Sort of like modern paintings?"

I think about it. "Yeah."

He takes a sip of coffee and grimaces.

"Bad?"

"Too cold. Anyway, modern paintings. They can be sort of indirect, right?"

"I guess."

"Like it isn't necessarily a picture of something recognizable."

"Right."

"But do you sometimes like looking at them

anyway? Do you stand in front of abstract paintings and let them wash over you?"

I think about a time at a museum in New Orleans with my mom when I was little. She held my hand as we walked past the big paintings. I remember staring at them, wide-eyed and curious. "Yes."

"If a poem is using words in a way that isn't quite what you're accustomed to, don't think that there's something wrong with you or your ability to understand them. They're just art objects painted with words. Sometimes they look like things you recognize, and sometimes not."

I'm still thinking of a painting from that museum. It was a violin and a bottle on a table, but it wasn't like looking at a violin and a bottle on a table. Even though my mom could only take me to the art museum on free admission days, going there made me feel like I was part of a species that could do something beautiful sometimes, even if it was only to *cry* beautifully.

"Show me something I haven't already seen." I don't know why I say it. I don't know where it came from.

The words seem to make Carlos very happy. "Exactly," he says.

I leave the observation lounge because being hungry makes the noise noisier and there are too many food smells driving me crazy.

I sit in my seat looking out the window instead.

I see some pronghorn antelope, a group of five, watching the train go by. Cows often run from the train, but the deer and now the antelope just watch it like it's something new and interesting.

The antelope have short horns and short tails, and they're just short all the way around. Looking at them standing in the yellow grass that isn't so tall, I decide that they're short because the grass is short, and the grass is what hides them from the things that want to eat them.

I decide this makes the antelope smart.

The light dims, the picture out the window turns the color of lavender, and I drift off to sleep.

I dream that I'm in Palm Springs at bingo night with Gramma. It's something that happened that has become a dream I have now and then. I don't know why I dream things from real life and then I dream them again. It's like I'm taking a class that I've flunked over and over again. But I don't think I flunked this thing.

Gramma liked bingo, which is a game where everyone has a card with squares that have numbers on them, except at this place they had easily recognizable objects like an apple or a dog. It's a bunch of old people, like a hundred on a busy night, and it's the closest thing to excitement at the manufactured housing community we lived in.

This particular night I sat at one of the long tables with Gramma on my left and an old man named Walter on my right. His wife, Betty, was on the other side of him.

An old lady with bluish hair spoke into the microphone. "All right, is everyone ready for some excitement?" There were a few enthusiastic responses. Walter mumbled something and looked around.

"Okay, you know the rules, winner gets half the pot, which tonight should be somewhere around forty dollars!"

I looked at Gramma, who licked her lips. No doubt she was thinking about a carton of menthols if she won the game. So was The Chevalier, who barked and then sat, trembling in Gramma's bag beneath the table.

The woman at the podium took the first card from a deck. "Okay, the first picture is *moon*. Does everyone remember what the moon is?"

There were some mumbled responses.

"It's that thing!" An old lady pointed at the ceiling. "That thing up in the sky!"

An old guy with no teeth started singing. *"Shine on, shine on, harvest moon . . ."*

Walter looked at me. A sound like Gramma's weak air-conditioning escaped his lips.

"There, Walter, *there*!" Betty shouted at him. She held a magnifying glass as big as a Ping-Pong paddle. "Right next to the hen, you fool!"

I looked at my sheet. There was a moon shining brightly right in the middle of it. I took one of my markers and put it on the square.

The blue-haired woman at the front drew another card. "Next picture is *dog*. Woof! Woof! Who's got a doggy?"

I had it, a nice-looking Dalmatian at lower left.

Walter looked under the table. Maybe he expected to see a dog there.

"Come on, Walter, look at your card!" his wife shouted. "I can't do both of them!"

"Gramma's hot tonight," Gramma said, and nudged me. Technically it wasn't yet night as the sun was far from down, even though it was winter. But old people tend to turn in early, from what I've learned.

"Next picture. *Flower*. Like a pretty flower given to you by your beau."

"Yes!" Gramma shouted.

"This card is blurry!" Betty shouted. "I want a new one!"

Walter put one of the red game markers on his tongue.

"It's not candy!" Betty shouted, and fished it from his mouth.

"Next picture. *Cup*. Please pour some more coffee in my cup!"

There it was, with steam rising from it at the upper right of my card.

Gramma shook her head, searching.

Betty cursed. Her eyes looked terrifying, bulging behind her magnifying glass. "You're hopeless, Walter!"

I looked at him. He wore a light blue shirt with marlins on it. I wondered whether Betty picked it for him or whether he chose it himself before his brain went soft. I considered the possibility he might have liked marlins at some point in his life.

"*Chair*," the caller continued. It went on and on. Betty kept yelling at Walter. Someone had a bathroom accident and there was a brief commotion. But the hard-core bingo players, including Gramma, didn't even look up from their cards.

"*Pencil*."

"*Monkey*."

Bingo, I thought. I put the marker in place and looked around. Then I slipped my card in front of Walter, and pulled his in front of me.

"Bingo!" I shouted. Everyone looked my way. "Walter got bingo!"

Betty looked dubiously at Walter. "Don't bother, he just covers everything with the markers since I won't let him eat them." She shouted it so everyone in the hall could hear.

"Well, I do have to check his card." The blue-haired woman got on her scooter chair and drove our way, bumping a couple of chairs as she did. She cleared the markers off Walter's card and put them back on as she went through the deck.

"We have a winner!" the blue-haired woman shouted, and reached into her pocket for a handful of confetti, which she threw into the air above Walter.

"He wasn't even paying attention," Betty grumbled.

Walter looked up with wonder as the confetti rained down on him.

It felt good to make that happen for Walter. He was so old, maybe it'd be the last time in his life confetti fell on him. He could go out on a high note.

I BOLT AWAKE and look at my SpongeBob watch, but it's still broken. I'm disoriented for a moment. There's no confetti, no Walter, no Gramma. I feel like I've been asleep a while. Dorothea isn't in the seat next to me, so I get up into the aisle.

The penguin conductor comes toward me.

"Do you know what time it is?" I ask.

He has an old-fashioned pocket watch and he loves to show it off, so he's happy when I ask him for the time.

"Well, young lady, we're somewhere near the end of New Mexico or the beginning of Colorado. Waiting on cattle trains to pass before we can move again." He tugs the chain, pulling the watch from his pocket, and flips it open with dramatic flair. "And the time is three minutes before nine, which is true in both New Mexico and Colorado."

That means it's time to play blackjack with the scouts—so I thank him and hurry toward the observation lounge, but slow down before I enter. Three scouts are sitting at a table, and I walk by, holding a magazine lent to me by another passenger.

"There she is! Hey, you playing or what?"

I stop and look at them over my shoulder. "Oh, right. I guess so." I act like it hasn't been on my mind, though I've been plotting to win their money all day. The boy who trapped me in the space between the coaches is conveniently sitting alone on one side, so I have to sit next to him. "What game are we playing again?"

"Blackjack," he says. "By the way, the name's Caleb. And that's Stinky, and that's Tenderchunks."

"Rider," I say, nodding at them.

Caleb slides two dollars in quarters to me. "The ante is twenty-five cents per hand."

"Got it," I say.

"Don't you wanna know why my name is Tenderchunks?" asks Tenderchunks.

"No," I say.

Stinky snorts. Caleb laughs.

Caleb shuffles the deck and deals the cards. I have a jack with a seven showing. Stinky has a two showing, and Tenderchunks has a queen showing.

Caleb has an ace showing, and he looks at his other card and smiles. "You should all just give me your money now," he says. "Stinky, you need a card?"

"Duh."

Caleb deals him a ten, and Stinky groans. He turns his cards over, revealing a king to go with his ten and two. He's busted.

"What about you, Tenderchunks?"

Tenderchunks looks at Caleb's ace. "I *know* you have twenty-one," he says.

"Cheater. You want a card or not?"

Tenderchunks grimaces and nods. Caleb throws down a seven. Tenderchunks curses and turns over his cards.

"You had twenty and asked for a card?" Caleb asks, smirking.

"I *know* you have twenty-one."

Caleb turns to face me. "Rider. Sweet little Rider. Seven showing. You need a card?"

I shake my head. "I'm good."

He looks at me like I'm stupid. "Really? Seven showing against my ace?"

"I'm good."

"Okay, then. Just so you know, when someone has an ace showing, there's a really good chance they have

73

twenty-one. There's, like, sixteen cards that are worth ten. And four that are worth nine, and four that are worth eight, and four that are worth seven—"

"I have one of the sevens."

"Are you counting cards?" he asks.

I shake my head.

He smirks again. He's big on smirking. "You feel lucky, do you?"

"I don't feel lucky at all."

"All right." He makes like he'll turn over his card, but doesn't. He takes a gulp of orange soda. "Maybe I'll just take another card." He deals himself a two. It doesn't seem to be what he was hoping for. He takes another card, a king. His lips move as he counts silently. He looks at me and turns over another card, a ten. He curses, busted at twenty-five. He turns over my cards.

"Argh! I can't believe you won with seventeen!"

The game goes on like this for an hour. I pay back Caleb the two dollars he lent me when he runs out of money. He loses that, then borrows money from Stinky and quickly loses that, too.

A scout leader in beige wearing a hat like Smokey Bear walks through the lounge, followed by a somber-looking blond kid holding a bugle.

"Okay, troops, time for 'Taps,'" the scout leader announces.

"You guys remember your tap shoes?" I ask, smiling.

"No," Stinky says, "'Taps' is when the bugler plays a song on the bugle and everyone has to be quiet after that."

"I know, I was just trying to humiliate you idiots." I get up to let Caleb out. As he tries to pass, he says quietly, "Maybe after 'Taps' I could meet you down by the luggage and play my guitar for you. No girl can resist my singing voice."

"Except me," I say. "Instead I'm gonna spend all this money at the snack counter. I'm gonna pig out."

Caleb looks crestfallen. He turns and follows his friends out of the lounge car.

"But thanks for asking," I call out after him. The door opens and closes, and in a moment I hear the miserable strains of "Taps" on the bugle.

I turn toward the stairs and Dorothea is standing there, blocking my way.

She doesn't look happy.

"Honey, is there something you'd like to tell me?"

I pause for a moment before I say, "Yes. Good night!"

She folds her arms. "There are reports that you and some of the scout boys were playing cards for money. *Real* money."

"Really?"

She doesn't smile. "You can't gamble on the train.

That's a violation of interstate commerce laws and federal gambling laws and I don't know what else."

"But I won. . . ."

"You need to give it back."

My shoulders sag. That keeps on happening with Dorothea. She's a real shoulder-sagger.

"You can't make me cry," I say.

"I don't wanna make you cry. I just want you to do what's right. Gambling is a serious thing. My uncle Rufus wrecked his marriage gambling away his paychecks."

"*Rufus*? Is he a dog?"

She shakes her head. "Just hand over what you won, and I'll make sure it gets back to the scouts you won it from." She holds out her hand, palm up.

I sigh, then dig into my jeans pocket three times to get all the quarters. She seems impressed.

"Now I gotta fill out a dang incident report," she says, and trudges off.

I slink down the stairs to the snack counter, feeling bad about being disrespectful to Dorothea, asking if Rufus was a dog.

"Hey, Nate. Are you still open?"

He smiles. "It's *Neal*. And no. But for you, yes."

"Really?"

"Sure. How'd it go?"

"I won a bunch of money from them. Like ten dollars in quarters."

"You were playing for money?"

"Of course! Why else would I hang out with those fools?"

"Well, I don't want to encourage you gambling. But, *nice*."

"You were right. I just trusted the formula. The scout boys made the mistakes you warned me against."

"A win for you is a win for all mankind," he says.

"I thought I'd celebrate with some M&M's. And maybe a veggie burger. And a bottle of water."

"Comin' right up." He turns to put the veggie burger in the microwave, then back to me. He grabs a handful of mayonnaise and mustard packets.

"Unfortunately, Dorothea made me give the money back."

He turns to me. "Really?"

"Yeah, she said it was against interstate commerce laws and federal gambling laws and all kinds of other laws."

Neal sighed. "I'm sure she's right. If there's one thing Dorothea knows it's rules."

I nod. "So I'm afraid I can't have the veggie burger and M&M's and water."

The microwave goes *ding*.

The ghost of a smile appears on his lips. "Yet there is a freshly nuked veggie burger waiting for someone to eat it."

"Maybe someone will come along who wants it. Someone with money?"

He turns and removes it from the microwave, and puts it on the tray. Then the M&M's and water. He pushes it closer to me.

I put my hand to my heart. "Really? You're the best."

"No, you are. Now get out of here so I can finish up. See you in Kansas tomorrow?"

I smile. "Is that where we'll be?"

"Yep. The Jayhawk State."

"See you in Kansas, then!" I grab my food and run up the stairs.

Back at my seat I balance the cardboard tray on my lap and examine my veggie burger. The bun is steamy and sticks to the patty as I peel it off. I open the mustard and mayonnaise packets and slather them on, replace the bun, and take a bite. It doesn't taste terrible, but the bun is hard at the edges and the patty is too chewy. I make quick work of it anyway.

The M&M's for dessert are perfect. I eat them one at a time, cracking the candy shells and letting the chocolate melt on my tongue.

As I eat them I think back to Palm Springs, where Dr. Lola would talk with me about how sometimes girls going through terrible times will get all boy crazy. Like, they'll start trying to get boys to notice them and to say nice things about them so they can forget their troubles and feel good about themselves. I wondered about that back then, and I wonder about it now as I sit eating M&M's one at a time, thinking about Neal and Caleb and letting the chocolate melt on my tongue.

Chocolate is good. Chocolate is safer than boys.

8

DOROTHEA TELLS ME we're almost in La Junta, Colorado, where we can get off the train and stretch our legs. This doesn't happen very often, so I decide to stay awake for it.

The cabin in the coach is dark except for the little lights that show on the aisle floor, and a couple of people that have their overhead lights on to read. I have my light on to keep me company.

I'm looking out the window at the black night when suddenly I see the reflection of Tenderchunks standing in the aisle. I turn to him.

"Hey," he says.

"Hey," I say. "Did you get your money back?"

"Yeah. But I wanna give mine back to you."

"Really? Why?"

He shrugs. "That woman is right about gambling. Some people are really hurt by it. But I think that's a lesson for next time. If we all did something we shouldn't have done, why are you the only one who gets punished? We get our money back and you have to give it. It doesn't seem fair."

I think about this, looking at him.

"So, here," he says, and extends a hand full of quarters. "This is five dollars, which is about what you won from me, but certainly less than what you won from all of us."

I look at his hand, and his arm, which is kind of veiny. He looks skinny but strong, like maybe he ties a lot of knots with thick rope, or chops wood or whatever it is the scouts do to kill time in the woods.

"Come on, take it," he says.

I make a cup of my hands and receive the coins, warm from his holding them.

"I gotta get back before they send a search party. I said I was using the latrine."

"Latrine?"

"You know. Bathroom."

I shake my head. "You guys are dorks."

He smiles again, then turns to leave.

"Thanks," I call out, but he's already gone.

I count the quarters, and it's five dollars like he said. I think that maybe I should give it to Neal and Amtrak for the food I ate since I didn't have money but now I do. But then I think how I'll be hungry again soon enough and I can use the money for more food.

The lights of La Junta appear in the dark windows. The train slows down, and a small station comes into view. It's not old and fancy like some of the stations. It reminds me of the dry cleaner in Palm Springs where Gramma went to clean the dress she wore at funerals.

Dorothea appears. "Come along, honey. Stay by my side, okay?"

"Yes ma'am," I say, all southern-like.

A conductor puts a plastic yellow step down at every door, and people step off and onto the platform, stretching, lighting cigarettes, ambling around. A few people are getting off for good and take their luggage with them. A few are getting on.

"See those Indian women?" Dorothea says. "Poor things. They sit there with the jewelry they make hoping to sell it to the people who get off the train to stretch their legs. But the train's so late, there ain't hardly anyone getting off, and the poor things been waitin' all day."

I look at the women and girls, sitting on the pavement with blankets spread before them, covered with jewelry. "Native Americans," I say quietly.

Dorothea looks at me and shakes her head. "You're right, you're right. I gotta stop callin' 'em Indians."

"Can I look?"

"Sure, honey. We got a few minutes."

I look over my shoulder at the train as if I expect to see it pulling away, then walk to the women and their jewelry. Dorothea walks beside me, checking her phone. I slowly move from left to right past the half dozen women, and then back to a little girl. She's maybe six, and has little bracelets made of tiny beads on thread in pretty designs.

"Did you make those?" I ask.

The girl looks to her mother, who says something to her in another language, then nods at me.

"How much?"

She holds up three fingers. I bend down to look more closely, and choose one. It has beads the color of the red dirt we've been seeing since we got to Arizona and New Mexico, and beads that are white like the fluffy clouds of the southwestern sky, and turquoise beads that are the color of nothing but turquoise.

"Can you help me tie it on?"

She looks to her mother, who takes it and ties it to my wrist. It looks nice. I smile at the girl, and she smiles at me. But she looks tired. I fish the five dollars in quarters from my other pocket and give all of it to her. She counts it and tries to give me back two dollars, but I tell her to keep it. She says something to me in her language and looks to her mother, who smiles.

"She says she likes your hair."

"Thank you," I say, and then look to the girl. "Thank you."

I don't think I ever needed to earn money by the time I was her age. I hope she sleeps well.

It has rained in La Junta earlier in the day, and the air smells good. Walking with Dorothea on the platform, I get goose bumps from how wonderful it smells. It reminds me of the smell when it rained in Palm Springs, which is different from the smell of rain in New Orleans. The rain smell makes everything seem new and full of possibilities. I fill my lungs with it as we walk from the back of the train to the front, then back again.

"We'll have a longer stop in Kansas City, whenever we get there," she says.

We head back toward our yellow step to board. I feel dreamy. I'm feeling good that I gave the little girl an extra two dollars.

We come upon Neal.

"Look," I say, holding up my arm to show the

bracelet. Then I remember it cost money I supposedly didn't have, so I hide it behind my back.

Neal sees me and smiles, and hides a lit cigarette behind *his* back.

I feel my brow furrow as I think about how people are always hiding things, and doing things they shouldn't do, things that hurt them and things that kill them and things they do anyway. I wonder whether the people who care about Neal worry about him dying from smoking. I wonder if anyone is worrying about me.

Back on the train, in my seat, I look at my new bracelet and think of the little girl who made it. It's tough for her to have to be out late, but at least she's with her mother. I'm constantly thinking about how easy or how hard the lives of others are, especially when I'm trying not to feel sorry for myself.

Back in Palm Springs, after Gramma died, Les and Ray took me in and I slept on their couch. But then a nosy neighbor named Eunice who didn't think it was right for me to be living with them reported me to Child Services, and they took me away from them and put me in a youth shelter. Most of the kids there had parents who were in jail or on drugs, and they stayed there waiting for their parents to get off drugs or out of jail, or for some better option to miraculously appear.

I had been in places like it before, back in New Orleans. Mom would get arrested, and I'd hang around a neighbor's apartment until they'd get sick of me and call the agency. Then I'd be in a shelter until Gramma coughed up the money to ship me out to Palm Springs. This happened a few times, going back and forth, each time Gramma making me feel bad about how much of her money she had to spend to send for me. And even though she hated paying the money to send me back, she'd be sick of having me around so she'd put me on the next bus as soon as my mom got out of jail, instead of waiting for my mom to come up with the money.

Then finally my mom died and there was no more back-and-forth. Dr. Lola hoped that when I was in Palm Springs to stay I'd be accepted by my classmates better, but it never worked out that way. I never really fit in.

The shelter I got sent to when they took me away from Les and Ray was called Tumbleweed Terrace. It was about a dozen portable buildings in a field of dust, but the food was okay, and they had books and board games. Les and Ray got to visit me, and they came every day for lunch the two weeks I was there. They'd bring me food that was even better than what they served at the shelter, and usually a piece of candy.

Almost every day someone new would show up to replace one or two who got taken somewhere else, usually back home. But there was one girl who had been there for three years. Her name was Espy, and she was exactly the same age as me. We were born on the very same day in the very same year.

Espy had long dark hair and a pretty smile. She liked to read like I did, and we spent a lot of time talking about books.

The more I got to know her, the more I liked her. Her mom was a drug addict but she could never get clean. Espy said her mom wanted her back but she couldn't quit long enough even for a supervised visit. Espy never stopped hoping, and she never unpacked her suitcase. Every time she did laundry, instead of hanging her clothes in the closet or putting them in a drawer, she'd fold them and put everything back in her suitcase, like any minute her mom would show up. But it had been three years.

After I was at the shelter for two weeks, word came that this distant great-uncle in Chicago would take me in. He was Gramma's older brother, and I'd scarcely heard a word about him. Picturing myself living with an older, man version of Gramma wasn't the kind of thing to make my heart soar.

Everyone at the shelter acted like it was a happy thing, a happy ending, but I preferred the idea of staying with Espy and having lunch with Les and Ray every day. Instead, they'd show up the next day with a lunch packed all pretty with a sweet note inside, and I'd be gone without a good-bye. And Espy would stay behind with her packed suitcase.

Back at my seat the coach is dark and the train rocks me to sleep.

I dream of my father, or the dream version of him anyway. I never knew him, but in my dream he is handsome, with a cleft chin. He dresses smartly, and smiles when I come into view. In *reality* I never come into view, because he was gone before I was born. He never knew I would exist. But in my dream he spots me in a crowd, because of my hair. He approaches me and tells me he's sorry, and I slap him. I slap him because saying he's sorry is too little, too late, and because he'll never be near enough for me to slap when I'm awake.

I wake up and it's dark in the coach, and dark out the window beyond the curtain. We're rolling slowly through a small town in southeastern Colorado. Bright floodlights illuminate tall grain elevators painted white, and a coyote the color of sand who watches us pass. He's more alone than any creature I've ever seen.

After the bright lights the darkness of the empty space that comes after is even darker, like the quiet that's quieter after an argument.

Dorothea is asleep beside me in the aisle seat. Her head is tilted back, mouth open.

I'm cold, so I zip up my hoodie as high as I can, and put my hands in the pockets. Then I lean in to Dorothea just a little, and close my eyes.

9

I CAN'T GET back to sleep. I'm thinking about the lonely coyote, and everything that's happened. My timeline stretches behind me, a chart of other people's mistakes and bad choices and sadness that put me in this seat on this train on this night.

I'm so cold from the air-conditioning, my teeth are chattering. I've been wearing jeans and my toast-and-jam T-shirt and hoodie ever since I got on the train in Palm Springs almost two days ago, but I'm still cold.

I slip past Dorothea into the aisle. From the overhead rack I take the silly little book, *The Sun Is Shining*, because it's the only book I have. The coach is mostly sleeping except for a couple of people who are working on their laptops or reading, so I make my way toward the light of the observation lounge.

Inside there are a couple of people sleeping stretched out on the floor between the side-facing seats and the windows. There are also a couple of people sitting in the booths, sleeping with their faces on the tables. A couple of people are awake at the tables, reading. One of them is Tenderchunks.

"Hey," I say, sitting down across from him.

He looks up from a scout manual. "Hey."

After I don't say anything else, he goes back to reading.

I notice for the first time that one of his eyes is higher than the other. His face is a little lopsided, like when the camera moves while you're taking a picture. "Is that some sort of lame scout bible?" I ask.

He takes off his glasses and closes the book. "No, it just tells you what you're supposed to do in different situations."

I fold my arms. "Sounds like a lame scout bible to me."

"Whatever."

I lean forward and speak quietly. "Does it teach you how to pee standing up?"

He laughs, even though I was trying to insult him. "No. It tells you how to start a fire and how to put it out, and what to do if you're on fire, and how to not get lost, and how to find your way when you *do* get lost. That kind of thing."

"You guys need all the help you can get, I suppose. And you need to allow girls into your little club. You've got too much testosterone."

"I agree."

I pause and look at him, surprised. "You do?"

"Yeah." He looks at me like he's stating the obvious. "It's like all the boys are cruel and they're pretending to be virtuous. But I feel like I'm gonna get beat up at any moment."

"Wow. I can't believe I'm hearing this from one of you."

"I don't speak for them. You're hearing it from *me*."

"Why are you in it, then?"

"My dad wanted me to join. I like camping and everything, I just don't like the boys and the uniforms. I mean, some of the guys are all right, but they need to be around some girls to keep them from being cruel and violent."

"Huh." I'm still shocked to be hearing this.

"Trail mix?" He offers a small bag.

"Thanks." I take a handful. "So, why are you called Tenderchunks?"

He lowers his voice. "Caleb and some of the bigger guys made me eat dog food a few hikes back."

"Why?"

"They thought it was funny. It was the troop leader's dog's food." He looks over his shoulder. "He wasn't happy about it."

"The dog or the troop leader?"

He laughs. "Both."

I shiver. "Why were you acting like you thought it was funny last night?"

He looks up and down the aisle again. "I have to act like I think it's funny or I look weak. I have to act like I wanted to eat dog food."

I look into his lopsided eyes, as sad as a mistreated puppy. "I thought *girls* were mean."

"We should make a pact," he says. "A non-cruelty pact."

"Between us?"

"Between us. And everyone we meet. Until it extends to everyone."

I smile. I hope it isn't a smirk, though I can feel a little doubt in the corner of my mouth. "You're a big thinker, huh?"

He shrugs. "You should read this." He takes a book from his backpack. It's a small volume of poems by Allen Ginsberg. *Howl.* "It's gonna change your life. But don't let Caleb see it."

"Why not?"

"He likes to punch me when he sees me with a book of poetry."

"Sounds like a sweet guy." I flip through it. "Thanks."

"What's your book?" he asks.

"It's nothing. It's for babies."

He reaches for it and fans the pages. A small photograph falls from it.

"Who's this?" He picks it up at the edges and examines it. "Is this your mother?"

I nod. I can feel my expressionlessness.

"She looks like you."

I scoff. "She looks nothing like me."

He looks at the picture and back to me. "She looks *exactly* like you."

"Hellooooo?" I hold out a lock of my bright-green hair to support my case.

He shakes his head. "That's just color. You look like twins born years apart."

I take the picture form him and stuff it back between the pages of the book.

"Whatever. I'm nothing like her."

"If you say so."

He's ready to drop it, but I can't. "It's just that I don't want to be like her."

He nods. "I understand."

I look into his lopsided eyes. "Maybe I'll tell you

about her some other time."

"Whenever you're ready."

After Tenderchunks leaves, I sit alone at the table and read *Howl*. I read the poem as we roll through the dark American night, quiet but for the times when we pass freight trains with their oil cars and flat cars and boxcars boxcars boxcars. I read the poem and it sometimes doesn't make any sense to me but I feel like I get it anyway. I have never heard the word *Moloch* until Mr. Ginsberg shouts it again and again and again. I've never heard or seen the word but I'm sure I've felt it. The whole thing is like something I've always felt but could never understand.

When I can't keep my eyes open any more I go back to my seat. I sleep as the train shimmies, rocking me.

I dream I am a poet and I spell my name *R-y-d-r*. Mr. Ginsberg sometimes spells the word *your* as *yr*, and does other things with words and language that make me feel wide awake when I read it. In my dream, spelling my name *Rydr* is the first bit of poetry I write.

10

I AWAKEN TO light in the coach and the train rolling on. I look at my SpongeBob watch but it's still broken.

Dorothea is somewhere else. I push aside the curtain and see corn for miles. The land is gently sloping, and there's corn on every bit of it.

My mom used to tell me that my hair was the color of corn silk. That's the light-blond stringy stuff that you pull away from corn on the cob before you cook it. She loved playing with my hair, running her fingers through it. She had the same hair but she never played with her own.

I told her that when she died I'd dye my hair green so she could spot me easily, looking down from heaven. I don't believe in heaven but I acted like I did for her sake, when she was sick. I don't think you can tell a person who's dying that you don't believe in heaven. She asked me to promise not to color it green, so I swore I wouldn't. But then I did anyway because I was mad at her for breaking so many promises herself. Like *I'll meet you here right after school.* Like *I promise I won't do drugs anymore.*

I turn away from the corn and stand to fetch my hearts-and-flowers bag. I brush my green hair even though I don't care. I take my toothbrush and go downstairs into a bathroom.

My face looks terrible in the mirror. I brush my teeth anyway.

I'm mad when I leave the bathroom, maybe more mad than when I entered it. I'm mad at my mom for her broken promises. I'm mad at my gramma for being mean and nasty. I'm mad at both of them for dying. I'm mad at Neal for smoking, because he can't be my father if he ends up dying from cigarettes. I'm mad because I'm hungry.

I go upstairs, down the aisle to the lounge car, then below to the snack counter. Neal is there and he smiles at me.

"Good morning, Rydr."

"Hey, Dick. Can you spot me a coffee?"

He can tell I'm not happy so he doesn't correct me on his name.

"How about a bowl of cornflakes, too?"

I scowl. "If I see any more corn I'll vomit." But almost immediately I wish I'd said yes to the corn-flakes.

He sets a coffee in front of me.

"Got a smoke?" I ask.

"Aren't you a little young to be smoking?" he replies.

"I can't wait to start," I say. "I'm gonna have a two-pack-a-day habit."

He puts his hands on the counter and stares at me. "Is this about you seeing me smoking last night in La Junta?"

"Were you? I didn't notice."

He smiles, just a little bit. Apparently I haven't succeeded in making him mad. So I take my coffee, turn, and leave, grabbing an orange from a bowl as I do. I walk away slowly, waiting to hear him call me out on stealing the orange, but he doesn't. I climb the stairs to the observation lounge.

I sit at a table to myself, one table away from Carlos. He's reading a novel.

"Good morning," he says.

I don't smile. Instead I raise one hand from the table in what isn't quite a wave. I don't look at him.

I inspect the orange in my hand. It has a bruise on it. I take the lid off my coffee and stir in three sugars and one cream, turning it the color of Dr. Lola's skin.

I blow on the surface and take a sip.

"My three daughters wouldn't even look at me at breakfast when they were your age," Carlos says.

I stare out the window. Obviously he's telling me he knows something I don't. Or that he's seen it all already and he's got me and every other kid my age figured out. "How nice for them," I say.

I'm not looking at him but I can tell by his voice that he's smiling. "Are you being sarcastic?"

I think about it for a second. I shake my head. I don't want to look at his kind face. "My orange has a bruise," I say, and I get up and leave my table.

I go downstairs to where the bruised orange came from. I don't look at Neal but I hold the orange in front of me, my arm extended. "This orange has a bruise."

"The stolen orange has a bruise? Maybe it happened during your getaway."

My arm falls to my side, and I look at the floor. "I'm sorry I took it. I was mad at you."

He sits on a barstool behind the counter. "Are you mad at me for smoking?"

I nod.

"I'm mad at myself," he says. "I wish I'd never started. And when I try to quit, after a few hours of not smoking it feels like smoking is the only thing in my life that's good."

"Really?"

"Yeah. That's what addiction does to you. My boyfriend always tells me if I love him I should show it by quitting."

My heart sinks. I don't know why. I guess my fantasy of him being married to my dead mom just got even more impossible. It was a stupid dream anyway. "What's your boyfriend's name?"

"Chuck."

I nod. "At Gramma's we had a gay couple for neighbors. Les and Ray. But Gramma had no clue they were gay. You could hear them playing the piano and singing 'cause everyone's walls were thin. Gramma complained about the noise, but I liked it."

Neal just watches me. That's also what shrinks do, and eventually you keep talking to fill the silence.

"It wasn't a trailer park," I continue. "It was more like manufactured housing. And Les and Ray had the nicest home in the community. I used to spend a lot of time at their place. They made me salads and smoothies and taught me about healthy eating. And they had a ton of books they let me borrow. It was like living next door to a library."

Again, he just waits for more.

"Gramma didn't have any books. Except a few *Reader's Digest* condensed books. And she had disgusting foods mainly. Except when she made pancakes. Hers were the best."

I can't tell whether he's bored or fascinated with what I'm saying. He has a faraway look on his face, like he's looking at me but inside me or through me. But I can't stop talking.

"I miss them. Les and Ray. They were my friends."

I'm afraid if I keep talking I'll say something stupid, so I turn away quickly and run up the stairs. I'm met at the top by an old lady who is on her way down. So I turn around and hurry back to Neal.

"I forgot to pay for this orange," I say.

"It's yours for a smile," he says.

I smile. Not on purpose, or for the orange. I just can't help it.

"Thank you for the orange."

"You are *so* welcome."

I wait for the old lady to get to the bottom of the stairs. I smile at her and rush to the top, then grab my coffee and sit across from Carlos.

"Wanna split this orange with me?" I ask.

"Only if you help me with these doughnut holes."

"Deal." I bite the orange to get the peel started, then remember I'm sharing. "Oops," I say, but Carlos laughs and I start peeling. "My gramma in Palm Springs had an orange tree but you couldn't eat 'em. They were ornamental oranges. The peels were bumpy and they were really sour. But you could make marmalade out of 'em. Gramma taught me."

"Thank you," Carlos says, accepting his half of the orange from me.

"They smelled good through the peel, though. And the blossoms that came in spring were amazing. Gramma would leave the windows open to fill the house with their smell."

"That sounds beautiful."

He's looking at me like he knows already, so I say it. "She's dead."

His head tilts forward a little. "I'm sorry."

"I was living with her for the past two years. Cigarettes killed her." I look out the window. The corn is so high, the roofs of barns look like they're floating on it.

"Every time you eat an orange you can remember her."

I look at Carlos and nod. I eat my half of the orange and wonder if that will be a happy thing or a sad thing.

11

AS IT'S MY third day on the train, I'm starting to stink. My deodorant doesn't mask it. If I was alone on the train it wouldn't bother me so much.

I go to see Neal at the snack bar, and stand at a safe distance, out of smelling range.

"So, how do people take showers on the train?"

He smiles. I take that as not a good sign.

"In coach, they take them before they get on and after they get off."

I nod as if it sounds reasonable, though it doesn't. I look at my not-very-clean fingernails while I wait to hear better news from him.

"You might do the old-fashioned *cat wash*."

"Doesn't that end with me coughing up a fur ball?"

He smiles again. "Ha. Hilarious, but no. It's where

you stand in the bathroom and use a series of wet paper towels and dry paper towels to strategically freshen up. It can make you feel a lot better."

I walk away feeling skeptical, and less than enthusiastic. I go into one of the bathrooms that has extra space where you can change a baby without worrying about dropping it into the abyss, and there's a little place you can sit where you aren't actually making skin contact with something that you pee into. Starting with a handful of soggy paper towels and a stack of dry paper towels, I sit on the cushiony seat and take off one shoe, wash and dry my foot, then slip my shoe back on and repeat with the other foot. I get new soggy paper towels and work my way up inside my clothes, washing and drying, until I am under my arms and behind my ears. I finish with my face, scrubbing it with hand soap and rinsing with more wet paper towels.

I put a fresh layer of strawberry deodorant under my arms and go back to see Neal.

He's ringing up an old man for a cup of coffee. "Feel better?"

"Fresh as a daisy."

The old man shuffles off and goes slowly up the steps. I watch him put his right foot on the first step, then join it with the left. Then his right foot on the second step, joined again with the left.

I have an idea. I look around the snack area. I pick up a price list for the snacks. "Can I take this with me?"

"Of course."

I look at Neal. He looks back.

"Can I borrow your hat?"

"For what?"

"To wear, of course. Don't worry, it's not like I have lice." I used to have lice all the time when I lived with my mom. She said it didn't mean we were poor and there wasn't anything to be ashamed of. But we *were* poor, and I was ashamed of that and of having lice.

"All right." He hands it over. "We used to have paper conductor hats that we gave to kids as souvenirs."

"This is better." I put it on. "How do I look?"

He tilts his head. "Very official. And the prettiest Amtrak employee ever."

I smile. "Thanks." I see a cheap ballpoint pen on his counter and reach for it while I watch his eyes. Then I run up the stairs.

Making my way through the coach cars, some of the passengers are still sleeping. Some have masks over their eyes, or they're curled up in all sorts of creative positions in their seats. Sometimes their arms or legs are sticking out in the aisle and I have to watch out for them when I walk past.

Dorothea is sleeping too. Which is perfect. She's sleeping in her seat with her head tilted back and her mouth open, a mask over her eyes. She looks like Zorro. She snores like a sawmill.

Finally I'm in the last car, at the back. It's the farthest point from the snack bar on the whole train. An older man sits alone on the right, reading a detective novel.

"Can I get you anything from the snack bar?" I try to sound cheerful and confident.

He looks up, smirks, then looks back to his novel.

"What do you got to eat?" someone says.

I look to the left, where a college-age guy wearing a backward baseball cap sits.

"Here's the price list." I hand it to him.

He looks it over. "Bro, five bucks for doughnut holes? They better be good."

"Bro, our doughnut holes are an exquisite culinary experience. They've been called 'the gems of the snack counter.'"

He reaches for his wallet and hands me a five. I take the cap off the pen and write *doughnut holes* on the palm of my hand. I smile and bow, then turn away.

I hurry downstairs to Neal.

"Back so soon?"

I grab a container of doughnut holes and set them

before him. Smiling, I hand him the five.

"Enjoy," he says.

I hurry back to the end of the last coach, where the guy with the backward baseball cap is playing a video game on his phone.

"Here you are, sir." I hold them in offering.

"Awesome. Just put 'em down there."

I put them on the empty seat next to him. He continues playing his video game.

"There is no charge for my service, and tips are entirely voluntary."

"Great."

I watch him for a moment. His phone is making a disgusting noise like a video game character is eating something gloppy. "Tips are considered in good taste, but not mandatory."

He ignores me.

"That means you don't have to tip me, though of course tips are always appreciated."

"I'm gonna take you up on the option of not tipping."

He still won't look at me. Then his video game makes a fart noise, and a stupid grin appears on his dumb face.

I keep my chin up, and turn from him. He can't make me cry.

I ask the next row of seats, and the next, and within

a half hour I have enough tips for a veggie burger. And long before Dorothea wakes up I have enough money to eat dinner in the dining car on the white tablecloths.

Before we pull into the station at Kansas City we spend a long time stuck outside of town refueling. We've been alongside a big river for a while.

There's lots of rust on everything, and the landscape has been getting greener and greener.

Finally we arrive at the station and get to jump off to stretch our legs. It's early afternoon. It's been raining here, and low clouds move past the tall buildings of Kansas City. Dorothea calls someone on her cell phone and asks about her dog while we walk on the platform. She's got a French bulldog that someone watches for her while she's away. She misses him terribly.

An Amish man wearing suspenders and a black hat runs up and back on the platform for exercise. He lifts his knees high in the air as he runs, his beard blowing in the breeze. Dorothea and I watch him and smile at each other.

I look for Neal but don't see him. I think that maybe he's found somewhere else to smoke so I *won't* see him.

After a while, the horn blows, and the passengers who have gotten off to stretch their legs turn back toward the train. Dorothea watches me as I watch them all leave the outside air, the breeze, the filtered sunlight, the Kansas City skyline, back up the yellow step to the carpeted aisle, the seats, and the windows with the view that rolls by like a travel documentary.

I take one last deep breath of fresh air before climbing back aboard. Dorothea follows behind me, picks up and stows away the yellow step, and the train begins to pull forward, pushing the continent behind us.

12

IT'S STILL AFTERNOON. I'm at my seat, reading *Howl*. It isn't a book for kids, but I'm not much of a kid anyway. Kids have parents. Kids don't have to come up with crazy ways to earn money to feed themselves.

We're stopped somewhere in Missouri, whose farms are less orderly than the ones in Kansas. The land is less flat and more tumbled, and there are big stretches of dark woods and lots of creeks.

I see Dorothea in the reflection of my window.

"Carlos wants to see you."

"Why?"

She looks at her fingernails. "He needs some help with the crosswords."

"I'm reading."

"I see that. But you should come and help him. He's lonely."

"Really?"

"Yeah. It'll make him happy if you do the crosswords with him. He likes your company."

I leave the book on my seat and follow Dorothea to the observation lounge. Carlos is sitting at a table with his back to me, and I drop into a chair across from him. The crossword is laid out on the table. He hasn't completed much of it yet.

"Hey," he says, smiling. "Thanks for joining me."

"It's my pleasure."

"It's a good thing I've got a book of these puzzles, 'cause the Mississippi River is going to be holding us up for a while."

"Really?"

"Yeah. Here's one I need you for: 'Sonic artists: *blank* Fire.'"

"Arcade."

He counts the spaces. "Yep. That works. I don't know what the heck it means, but it works." He glances over my shoulder. "So, the Mississippi is so high it's lapping at the tracks in Fort Madison, Iowa. That's where we cross it, or where we would if we *could*. We have to wait for the river to back away from the tracks. Maybe a day or more."

"Really?" I immediately wonder how I'll manage to eat.

"It's like extra innings in baseball." Then Carlos cracks a smile and at first I think he's kidding about the river. But then the lights go dim, and I hear Dorothea and Neal singing.

It's my birthday, and they're singing "Happy Birthday" to me. By the time they reach the second line, half the observation lounge is singing with them.

They appear from behind me, Neal holding a cake with thirteen lit candles, illuminating their happy faces.

I start crying, 'cause it's the most beautiful cake I've ever seen, with pink and white frosting, and *Happy Birthday, Rider* written in fancy cursive.

They're done singing, and the candles are glowing. "Make a wish!" Dorothea says. But all I can do is cry. I'm shaking with it. I can't even draw a breath to blow out the candles. Dorothea pats me on the back. Neal sits down next to Carlos, and they're both smiling at me. I start pulling the candles from the frosting, dropping them into Carlos's coffee to extinguish them. He laughs.

"Those are happy tears, right?" Neal asks.

"I don't cry," I say, my voice sounding tortured. Everyone laughs. Finally I have dropped all thirteen candles into Carlos's coffee.

"I hope your wish comes true," Dorothea says.

My wish is for Espy, my friend from the shelter in Palm Springs. Today is her birthday too, and my wish is for Espy's mom to get clean so she can take her back. My wish is for Espy's suitcase to get unpacked in her own home.

Dorothea turns the lights back on, and sets down a stack of paper plates and forks. "I saw on your identification that you'd be having a birthday on the train. I mentioned it to Carlos and he ordered the cake from a bakery in Kansas City. They had it ready when we got there."

I look at Carlos, but I can't even manage to say thanks. I can't get the words out.

"Already this is the best birthday party I've ever been to," Carlos says. "Thank you for letting us celebrate it with you."

We eat the cake. It's white cake, it's the best cake, the best cake ever. I'll never forget how it looks, how it tastes. I can't say a single thing to anyone, but I'm filled with a supreme happiness, and a little bit of guilt for noticing that nobody ever threw me a birthday party that made me feel this good before.

The people sitting at the table with me feel like a family. *My* family. If I could choose my family they'd be just like this. This is how families should make each other feel on birthdays. No paramedics, no drama, no disappointments.

Only after three slices of cake and two cups of coffee can I manage the words *thank you.*

I'm a teenager now. But that's not why I feel different. I don't know exactly what it is, but I think it has something to do with this train I ride.

I walk downstairs to one of the bathrooms and look at myself in the mirror. I stare for a while.

"Hello," I say.

"Hello," the girl in the mirror replies.

"You are my daughter," I say. I tell her this frequently, and she always says the same to me. Dr. Lola thought it was a good exercise, and though it sounded pathetic at first, I ended up agreeing with her.

She looks not so much sad, but like she's been sad lots of times. But every now and then, happy. She has a little bit of cake frosting above her lip, which makes me smile to see, which makes her smile, and she licks it off.

"I trust you," I say to her.

"I trust you, too," she says.

"Remember last year? It started out as the worst birthday ever."

"Yes," the girl in the mirror answers. "Dead mom,

no dad, no friends. Only a grumpy gramma with a cupcake from the grocery store and a single candle she lit with her cigarette."

"Then Les and Ray stole you away from Gramma's."

I smile. "They got a princess cake and tiara. And they dressed like two jesters."

"You told them twelve was too old to be a princess."

"I know," I say. "But I was glad to be princess for a day."

"It ended up being the best birthday ever," she says.

"Yes. Until today."

She wipes her eyes on her shirtsleeve, then smiles. I wish her a happy birthday, and she wishes me the same. Then we blow each other kisses, and I leave her.

I walk upstairs, across and back downstairs to see Neal at the snack counter.

"Hello, beautiful," he says.

"Hello, handsome." I look at my shoes and then back to him. "I'm not really going to Disneyland."

"I'm glad, 'cause it's the other direction."

"My gramma died. That's why I'm on this train."

He nods, and takes off his cap. "I'm sorry."

"I was living with her for two years after my mom died."

His hand goes to his heart. He seems to be searching

for words but nothing comes out.

I look at his beautiful dark hair. "I don't want you to feel bad. I just don't want to be dishonest about it because it's nothing to be ashamed of."

"Are you going to your grandmother's funeral?"

I shake my head. "It already happened." I kick at the carpet. "I didn't really like her very much. But she kept me alive, especially when my mom couldn't."

Neal nods, a faraway look on his face. "Sometimes that's how it is."

I look at my fingernails. "Also, my name is spelled R-Y-D-R. 'Cause I say so."

I don't know why but he puts his hand to his mouth, like he's covering a smile. His eyes shine.

"I'm not the bad things that have happened to me," I say. "I'm nothing but who I choose to be."

"Yes," he says. "You've chosen well."

The train rolls on but it isn't in a hurry. It knows that it has to stop and wait at the Mississippi River, which we can't cross until at least tomorrow. We should have been in Chicago already but we aren't even in Illinois yet, thanks to the delays.

I don't care. Let it rain. Let the river rise and wash

away the tracks that would take me to Chicago.

Tenderchunks passes through my coach, nods at me, and heads downstairs. I count to five and follow after him.

At the bottom of the stairs are a few bathrooms. I stand halfway from the bottom and wait until I hear the sound of a bathroom door opening, and then descend.

It's just a man with a beer belly. I turn sideways to let him pass, then go back up a few steps. Another door opens, and this time it's Tenderchunks.

"Oh, hey," I say.

"Hey."

I'm standing square in the narrow stairway, blocking him. "So, I thought I'd eat in the dining car tonight." I glance down at my dead SpongeBob watch. "I'm kinda sick of doughnut holes and veggie burgers. But you have to have two people to get a table."

"Really?"

I nod. "Yeah. And since you're pretty much the only scout capable of conversation, I thought maybe you could be the other person."

"The other person?"

"You follow quick. Yeah, the other person. So I can eat there."

"Your invitation for me to be *the other person* is

extremely flattering. But I don't have enough money. That food is pretty expensive."

"Right. Well, it just so happens I made enough money delivering food today to pay for both of us." I'm standing two stairs above him, looking down.

"Do I have to pay you back?"

I roll my eyes. "No. Look, I'm sure I can find someone else—"

"I'd love to."

It takes me a second to figure out what comes next. I glance again at my broken watch, broken since the day I fought off the bully girls. My heart is racing now. "Okay. I'll meet you in the dining car at six thirty."

I'm having dinner with a boy. I think this is okay and maybe even good. Maybe I won't know until after it's over.

I SIT WITH Tenderchunks in the dining car at dinner. His goon squad is eating freeze-dried scout kibble from foil pouches in the observation lounge and at their seats, but he's sitting with me in the land of white tablecloths, waiting on a delicious meal.

Dorothea is at the table across the aisle, eating a mopey-looking sandwich from a Tupperware container. She says she has to be there because it's her job to watch me, especially if I am having dinner with a boy.

Tenderchunks puts the white napkin on his lap.

"What's your mom like?" I ask.

He's looking rather cute, with his scout bandanna tied loosely beneath his neck.

"I don't know. She's okay, I guess."

His left eye—the one that's a little higher—has a tendency to drift to the center. I decide I'll maintain contact with the right eye.

"Just okay?"

He looks out the window for a second. "I guess she's pretty cool. I mean, I love her, but she's my boss. It's a constant source of conflict. You know?"

I *don't* know, but I nod anyway.

"What's *your* mom like?" he asks.

"Dead." I say it flatly, and I feel bad for the look on his face. I probably shouldn't have blurted it out like that.

"Oh my gosh. How?"

I look at him and think about spilling it. I think about how I should just tell him my mom was a junkie and died from an overdose. Instead I answer the follow-up question. "And my father is a mystery."

"A mystery?"

"Meaning I have no idea who or what he is, or whether he's even alive." I take a sip of water. "He probably isn't."

"Who do you live with?"

"I was living with my gramma. But she died too. But now I'm going to a fabulous new life in Chicago." I say it brightly.

"Really?"

"No. I'm being shipped off to live with an old man I've never met. My great-uncle. He needs to stay alive for five years or I go into foster care."

Tenderchunks gets this miserable look on his face that people get when they ask about my life. "I'm . . . I—"

"You're not asking the wrong questions," I say. "You're just sitting with the wrong girl."

The server approaches our table with two plates of food, but it isn't ours and she keeps walking past.

"I'm pretty sure I'm not sitting with the wrong girl," he says.

I smile. I want to tell him he's nice, but I don't.

We both glance out the window. Then, fortunately, he changes the subject. "Have you started reading *Howl*?"

"Yeah. It's really long for a poem, but I've finished it. Twice."

He looks excited about this. "What do you think of it?"

"I can't get it out of my head."

"Really?"

"Yeah. The chanting made me feel like I was hypnotized. And what he talks about. It's everything wonderful and terrible. It's the world I've seen my whole life. I didn't know anyone else saw what I've seen."

"Good. That's good." He takes a sip of water.

"What's *Moloch*?"

He looks even more excited that I've said a word from the poem, proof that I really *have* read it.

"Moloch is, like, this terrible ancient god that people sacrificed their children to. The whole poem is about how maybe the best kinds of people are the people who fail and go crazy. Like, the problem isn't the people, the problem is what they're supposed to do."

I nod, but I'm quiet for a minute. This is a revelation to me. That the *misfits* are the best people. That there's nothing wrong with the people who can't survive. It's the world that destroys them that needs to be fixed.

"So, what do you think of it?" he asks.

"I'm going to need to read it again."

He grins. "You're gonna read it over and over for the rest of your life."

I feel like I'm not wearing any clothes. Like he understands me better than I understand myself. "How do you know?"

"I can tell. There's a light in your eyes."

I take a sip of water from the heavy glass. "A light?"

A plate appears before me. It's a big white plate loaded with food, and when the server sets it down, there's heat rising from the asparagus and fries that accompany my humongous portobello sandwich. I look at it in disbelief.

Tenderchunks's food arrives too, and as we start to eat I can't tell whether the strange feeling in my stomach is coming from the first real food I've had in days, or the revelation that there's a light in my eyes.

The reservations are only for forty minutes so we have to leave to make way for the next table. And Tenderchunks has to go to the observation lounge, which the scouts have basically commandeered for some ridiculous wood-whittling instruction.

I spend this time in my seat, thinking about writing in my journal, but I don't. My head gets noisy so I head toward the snack counter to see Neal. As I pass through the observation lounge, Caleb and the other scouts stare at me. Someone nudges Tenderchunks, and he looks up and smiles. I wink at him, making sure that Caleb and the others can see.

Downstairs in front of Neal, I don't know what to say. So I say hi.

"Hi," he says. "What's shaking?"

"Shaking?"

"You know." He does a little dance.

I shrug. "I just came down to say hi."

"Are you hungry?"

"No, I just had dinner in the dining car." I look at my fingernails. "With Tenderchunks."

"*Ahhh.*"

"What?"

"Nothing. Was it nice?"

"Yes. But not nice like *that.*"

"Nice like what?"

"It wasn't like a date. We're not, like, in *love.*"

"Not in love?" He smiles.

"Never mind. Nothing."

I wave good-bye to Neal and go back up and through the observation lounge. This time I keep my eyes to myself but I can feel theirs on me, the scouts, and I am suddenly aware of my hips, which seem to have a way of swaying when I walk, which I hadn't noticed before. The scout leader stops talking like he's lost their attention.

I feel my powers, my charms. I have dominion over boys.

Back in my coach, at my seat, I think of Dr. Lola's words. *Boy crazy.*

I reach up and feel my hair, wondering what it looked like when I walked through the observation lounge.

This is stupid. There's only one boy I want looking at me.

I take a deep breath, hold it, let it out. A deep breath,

hold it, let it out. I don't know how long I do this before I fall asleep.

I dream I am camping with Tenderchunks. We've hiked for days and have run out of food. He's looking in his scout guide and reading the suggestions aloud, but there's nothing in there to help us. Just some pages about hair stew and having your friends for dinner.

We're starving.

We're in the middle of a big plain as vast as the grasses of New Mexico. There's nothing but trampled yellow blades, nothing to eat. The sun sinks and the sky fills with color, then goes dark. Tenderchunks says good night to me and zips himself into his sleeping bag.

I stay up all night in the dream, facing the point on the horizon where the sun vanished, watching the stars move in the sky. They move very fast, like stars in time-lapse photography. Like science class.

Then the sun comes up on the other side of the sky, behind me, and illuminates a sea of portobello mushrooms that have sprouted overnight. They are everywhere, as far as I can see.

I wake up Tenderchunks. "It's a miracle!" he says,

and laughs. "It was our only hope! Now we can make portobello burgers!" He takes a bag of hamburger buns from his backpack, and I wonder why we didn't just eat the buns if we had them and we were so hungry.

"Is this a dream?" I ask.

He hands me a portobello burger. "Does this taste like a dream?"

I take a bite. It tastes like a dream. It tastes like a dream where I trust my instincts and everything works out okay.

My head snaps back and my eyes open. It's dark in the coach.

I slip past Dorothea's sleeping form and into the aisle, and hurry to the observation lounge. Tenderchunks isn't there.

I'm broke again after paying for dinner for me and Tenderchunks. Schemes present themselves in my mind.

There's a guy with a book bag at another table. I borrow a pen from him and make a sign on a napkin. It says *Your future foretold! Tips accepted.*

I sit at a table with my sign in front of me. Nobody is coming or going.

Finally some of the scouts come in, quieter than they usually are, presumably because it's after "Taps" and they aren't supposed to be out of their seats.

I feel my heart beating. Tenderchunks is among the four.

"Look, it's sweet little Rydr," Caleb says.

My eyes are half-closed, fingertips to my temples. "Silence! I'm having a vision."

He looks down at my sign. "Desperate for money again?"

I open my eyes. "No. I have a gift that presents itself when magnetic conditions are favorable, and I try to share it with those brave enough to peer into the future."

I give Tenderchunks a small wink.

Caleb looks askance at me. "And it doesn't cost anything?"

"Tips are accepted." I clear my throat. "But in your case, prepayment is required to clear the hostile mists of uncertainty."

He scoffs. "What a bunch of garbage."

I shrug. "That's what the pilot said to me. And then I saw the news." I lower my eyes and try to do the sign-of-the-cross thing that Catholics do.

"Whatever. How much?"

I close my eyes and move my lips as if I'm consulting

the spirits. Really I'm remembering how much a bag of M&Ms cost at the snack counter. "Three dollars."

He fishes in his pocket and finds the quarters I won from him once before. It's good to have them back.

"Sit," I say, and nod at the seat across from me. Caleb sits across and the others crowd in—Tenderchunks, Stinky, and a kid called Wispy. "Hold out your hand." He does. I hold it in mine and trace the lines with my fingertip. I look up at Caleb's handsome face. "You've never done any hard work, have you?"

"Says who?"

"Says the soft, tissue-thin skin of your palm. It's like a baby's butt." One of them suppresses a laugh. I look back to Caleb's hand. I close my eyes, and speak in a faraway voice. *"Bed-wetter."*

Stinky snorts and Caleb elbows him in the ribs.

"What?" I ask. "Did the spirit communicate through me?"

"What else does it say?" Wispy asks.

I close my eyes again. I can feel someone's shoe on mine under the table. I growl my foretelling. *"Beauty fades, leaving nothing!"* Then I shudder and open my eyes.

Stinky laughs again, and Caleb pushes him into the aisle.

Then the scout leader appears in the doorway. He's wearing his Smokey Bear hat even though we're inside a train. He blows a whistle, which I'm sure doesn't sound pleasant to the people sleeping in the observation lounge and the next car.

The scouts tumble out of the booth like it's on fire.

I laugh. "Doomed! All of you!"

I was hoping to get a chance to hold Tenderchunks's hand and tell him *his* fortune. I'd tell him that in spite of what it says in *Howl*, the best minds of *his* generation aren't always destroyed by madness, that sometimes the best minds get lucky. I'd tell him that he'd find love while on a journey, or that maybe he'd found it already. I'd tell him this while holding his hand and feeling the blood come and go with the beating of his heart.

Instead I have to settle for a quick smile as he leaves.

I sit in the observation car, hoping Tenderchunks will come back alone. I wait for a while until I feel pathetic and needy, then get up and head to my seat.

I run into him in the vestibule. The door he came through closes, then the door I came through closes. We're there in the little space between the coaches, where the noise of the train is louder. Another scout encountered here, but this time it's the right scout.

"Hey," he says.

"Hey," I reply. "Where are you headed?"

"To find you."

This makes me want to smile, but I'm afraid I'll look stupid if I do.

"Here I am."

He smiles. The train shimmies back and forth.

"How did you get into poetry?" I ask out of nowhere.

His face turns down. He covers his grin.

"What?" I ask.

"Nothing. Well, first it was Walt Whitman. We had to read *Leaves of Grass* in English class. It's this *huge* poem." He spreads his arms wide and gets this faraway look on his face.

"And you liked it?"

"I *loved* it. It was the first time I read anything that made me . . ."

"What?"

He shakes his head. "It's the whole continent. It's all of life stuffed into one little volume."

I nod. "And that's good?"

"Yeah. It's like borrowing a great set of eyes. A wonderful, wise set of eyes."

"I'll read that next," I say.

He takes off his glasses and starts laughing, then wipes his brow.

"What?" I ask.

He smiles, but he doesn't look at me straight on. "I'm in this small space with a beautiful girl, talking about poetry. It's like a dream."

"A dream?" I ask. Then I understand what he's really saying. *"Oh."*

The train shudders, and I lose my balance and fall forward. He puts out his hands and steadies me.

"Thanks," I say.

His face is inches away. His good eye is looking at me, the other is gazing off to the side like it's distracted by something else.

I can practically feel the vibration of his voice when he speaks. "If we lived in the same town I'd wanna hang out with you."

"I'd let you," I say, and my voice sounds funny. I feel like I want to breathe the breath he's breathing.

My chin tilts up. It gets dimmer, like my eyes are closing.

Then the door slides open noisily. Dorothea is standing there. She doesn't look mad. She looks really calm, which is sort of scary.

"It's time to say good night to your friend," she says.

I turn to the face inches from mine. "Good night," I say.

"Good night," he answers. He turns and bows

slightly to Dorothea as he goes through the door.

I sigh. "Are you gonna yell at me?" I ask.

"Have I yelled at you yet?"

I think about it. "No."

She nods. "He seems like a nice boy."

"He is."

We leave the vestibule, and Dorothea leads me back to our seats. I sit by the dark window, she sits on the aisle.

"I was watching the two of you for a minute," she says.

"You were?"

"Through the window of the door." She smiles, kicks off her shoes. "I let you have as much time alone as I could. But I couldn't let you kiss him."

"I *wasn't* gonna kiss him."

She chuckles. "Oh yes you were."

"I was?"

She nods, eyes closed and smiling.

I close my eyes and think about how I almost kissed a boy without even knowing it was about to happen. It's scary, but it's not so scary because of who the boy was.

I think of the almost-kiss, and I think of the portobello dream I had earlier, hoping I can return to where it left off.

The train rolls on into the vast darkness.

Instead of falling asleep I fall into a memory. It's a memory that plays in my head all the time, like there's something I need to learn from it that I haven't.

I'm at school in Palm Springs, trying to open my locker.

These girls who always pick on me come up and form a half circle around me.

"Where's your mommy?" the loudest one says. "Is she soaking her dentures?"

I try to ignore her. I have my back to them, trying to get my algebra book out of my locker, but I can't seem to get the lock combination right.

"Maybe she's playing bingo with the other old people where you live?"

The other girls laugh.

"She's not my mom. She's my gramma."

The girls laugh while I tug on the lock. It won't open.

"Then where's your *mommy*? Didn't she want you anymore?"

I spin around. *"Shut up."*

There's four of them. My breathing is shallow.

The loud one pokes me in the chest. "What did you say?" She moves in. She isn't the beautiful golden-haired mean girl like in the movies. In fact it's sad how homely she is, and I almost feel sorry for her in this moment. "I asked you a question, freak! What did you say to me?"

I tell her to shut up again, but I add a word I'd never said before.

She slams me against my locker and I bounce back at her. I start swinging, punching at her. My unrecognizable fists are sped up like the fast forward on a movie. There is blood coming from her nose, she falls away.

I don't want it to happen but the other girls come at me. I see hands and fingernails and faces, and I see my fists.

It clears quickly. Big arms wrap around me. I hear myself breathing like a saw going back and forth.

There's one boy looking at me with surprise. Everyone else is a sea of blurry faces except this one boy whom I don't recognize, looking speechless.

I'm pushed along with my hands held behind my back, like I'm arrested.

The fluorescent lights in the office, the expressions on the faces of the school secretary and the principal. Everyone's a stranger, and none more than myself.

Someone holds an inhaler to my mouth. I breathe in.

I wait with the security guard. I look at my

SpongeBob watch and see the glass is broken, and the second hand has stopped moving. The fish in the tank looks worried.

They move me into Dr. Lola's office.

"Honey, what happened?" Dr. Lola cleans the blood from my knuckles with peroxide, revealing teeth marks. Her hands tremble as she wraps mine in gauze. She attends to everywhere else I hurt: the scratches on my face, the kicks to my legs. She gets my blood on her pretty skirt.

I throw up. I say I'm sorry.

A train roars by in the opposite direction, opening the shades of my eyes, bringing me back to where I am, in the dark night on the train. I wrap my arms around myself, then lean into Dorothea.

Those mean girls are far behind me, and so is the girl they picked on, that version of myself. Far behind me too is Dr. Lola, and that's what makes me shut my eyes against the pain.

14

I AWAKE TO Dorothea pushing my shoulder. I feel like I haven't slept so long in years, but my heart aches for Dr. Lola.

"Honey, the scouts are getting off in a few minutes. If you'd like to say good-bye to your friend, he's waiting for you in the observation lounge."

I nod, stand up quickly, then grab my bag to brush my hair. I brush my teeth without water, swallowing the toothpaste because there isn't time to go to the bathroom. Then I put some cherry ChapStick on my lips. My good-bye with Dr. Lola was all wrong. I don't want it to be wrong with Tenderchunks.

He waits for me at a table in the observation lounge, sitting next to his backpack. I drop in across from him.

"Hey," I say.

"Hey."

"So . . ."

"Our bus crossed the river downstream and it's picking us up on some country road. That's where the train is headed right now."

I don't want to feel this, this losing someone else, or for him to see me feel it. So I do the tough-girl act. "I'm stealing *Howl* from you. Hopefully you'll get over it."

He opens his mouth but doesn't say anything. He folds his hands and looks out the window, and then across at me. "Okay."

"Thanks."

He pauses again, then says, "So, I've been wanting to say that I like your dimples."

I reach up to touch where they would be if I was smiling. I wonder at what point I've smiled and caused them to appear for him to see.

"Did your mom have dimples?" he asks.

"No," I say, and accidentally smile just a little, because I'm nothing like her.

"There they are," he says.

I reach up to them.

He shakes his head. "They kill me. They're like arrows to my heart. It isn't fair."

I smile again. "I've seen the best boy of my generation destroyed by dimples." That's almost a line from *Howl*.

It has the intended effect on Tenderchunks. He looks incredibly happy that I've sort of quoted the poem.

"So, it would be nice to stay in touch with you," he says. "Are you on Facebook?"

"No. I've never really had a computer to use. And I don't even know what my address will be in Chicago. Somebody in a uniform is going to meet me at the station and take me somewhere else."

He cracks his knuckles, then puts his hands under the table.

"But I can look you up," I say. "Eventually. I mean, there aren't many people named Tenderchunks, right?"

He smiles. "I'll write it down for you. My real name and address."

"No, I could lose it. Whisper it to me."

I lean forward and turn my head. He moves in and I feel his breath on my ear. He whispers it to me—name, address with street number, town, and zip code. Then he says something else that gives me goose bumps.

"You promise you'll remember it?"

"It sounds like a lovely dream. I won't forget it."

The train slows down. He looks over my shoulder. I turn and see the scoutmaster at the doorway, giving him the stink eye.

"Well, it looks like I gotta go."

I point to his scout shirt. "What happened to the patches?"

"The merit badges? I took them off."

"Why?"

He glances out the window. "What do the troop leaders know about merit?"

I stare at him. "Can I have it?"

"My shirt?"

"Yeah. To remember you by?" It's a lie, because there's no way I'm forgetting him, with or without his shirt.

He looks down and starts unbuttoning his shirt, and puts it on the table in front of me. He's left wearing a white undershirt.

I reach for my wrist. "You can have my SpongeBob watch. It's busted, but it died a hero. It broke when I was fighting off four girls who were picking on me."

"Wow." He puts it on. "This is gonna give me strength."

"Nobody can ever make you eat dog food again." I put on his scout shirt and button it up. "How do I look?"

"I'd stay in scouting for that."

"Are you leaving it, then?"

He shrugs. "Maybe I can get my dad to go camping with me instead."

I clear my throat. I feel my lungs tightening but I'm not gonna let it happen. I'm not gonna let an asthma attack ruin this moment. "I'd kiss you except I don't really do that. I try not to get my sense of self-worth from boys."

He nods. "That's smart."

"But maybe next time I see you."

He moves to the aisle and shoulders his backpack.

I stand and put myself between him and the scoutmaster. "Well, good-bye." I hold out my hand.

He shakes it. "Good-bye."

I close my eyes for a whole second. Then I lean in and kiss him on the cheek. "I didn't need to do that," I say. "I'm feeling pretty good about myself right now, but you looked like you needed a kiss."

"You're right." His eyes are watery.

"You should probably dry your eyes before Caleb sees you."

He nods and pauses, then leans in and kisses me, right on the lips. Then he moves past me and walks away down the aisle with tears rolling off his face, ignoring my advice. I watch him go, mouthing his name and address to myself, and everything else he whispered, burning it into my memory.

Then I run through the train to fetch my journal so I can write it down, just in case I lose my mind.

15

WE'VE BEEN OUTSIDE Fort Madison, Iowa, since last night. Now it's afternoon, and I'm tired of looking at the same view, even if it's a *nice* view. Outside my window is a field of soybeans, which have a way of moving in the breeze, like endless tiny waves, that's very pretty to see. Beyond them, wind turbines spin in the distance. But I want the train to go backward, to keep it from getting to Chicago and emptying out all the people I've met on board. I want it to bring me back to where Tenderchunks was on the train.

After the Mississippi River retreats from the tracks, they have to check everything and make sure it's safe. That's what Dorothea says.

When we finally start moving again it will be only a matter of a few hours before the train stops and I get off.

I stand and look in my hearts-and-flowers bag. I take the deodorant out and put some under my arms. I put on some cherry ChapStick. Nobody cares about my lips but it tastes good.

I rehearse Tenderchunks's name and address just in case I lose my journal. Over and over I say it in my head just to make sure it's still there.

I think about drawing him but I'm not so good at drawing people. Even if I was, I couldn't do him justice.

I sit back down. I fidget with the loose threads where the merit badges had been on the beige scout shirt I'm wearing. I picture myself making him a new set of badges and imagine what they'd be for. *This one's for being true to yourself. This one's for being a free thinker.* His smell is still on the shirt. *This one's for being a good kisser.*

I find myself wishing I could tell my mom about him. Gramma wouldn't have wanted to know anything about my meeting a princely boy, but Mom would have. And then I think of Mom, and her face. Sometimes I wonder if I'll ever forget her face or the sound of her voice, and I wonder if I really care whether I forget. But then I feel bad about thinking that. And I remember that Tenderchunks and everyone else says I look exactly like her, except my dimples, which only show on the rare occasions that I smile. So all I have to do is look in the mirror.

The shrinks and social workers say she had a disease, that it's just like cancer, that she didn't choose to be who she was. That she had a mental thing that she medicated as best she could.

But not everyone saw it that way. Gramma said bad things about her all the time, and when she did I'd get mad at her and say, *How dare you talk about my mom that way.* Even if I had been thinking the exact same thing right before Gramma said it.

When I see someone like Neal, who smokes even though it's bad for him and it might kill him and his boyfriend begs him to quit, it makes me feel like I understand my mom better, but it doesn't keep it from hurting.

I don't even like saying what it is, or thinking about it. But when I have my thoughts to myself, like at this moment staring at all the soggy fields of soybeans and corn outside Fort Madison, Iowa, waiting for a giant river to exhale, it gets noisy in my head. It gets noisy in my head and I worry that I'm the same as her. Doomed.

Since before I was born she was that way. She didn't even mean to have me. I was a mistake. She'd say she loved me but her actions told a different story, and there was no getting around the fact that I was a mistake. I was one of hundreds of mistakes she made, but I was the one that stayed around, looking at her, needing her, reminding her what she was, and how far short of the mark she fell from where she needed to be, and who she wanted to be.

I was back and forth between my mom and Gramma. Mom would pull herself together and I'd live with her, and then she'd screw up and I'd have to go back to Gramma. I got sick of being disappointed. I felt like I couldn't feel anything anymore, and I didn't want to.

Then she got sick and we thought she would die. That's when I told her I'd dye my hair green so she could spot me from heaven, even though I don't believe in heaven and I'm pretty sure that if there was such a place, they wouldn't let in people who can't take care of their daughters. Then she sort of got better, she looked better, her liver worked again, and I was dumb enough to think she'd learned her lesson.

I was the one to find her.

I can't even say it.

I can't say the words.

I can't say *needle*.

I can't say *blood*.

I can't say *blue-faced*.

I can't say *dead eyes*.

Even before she died, I was always a motherless child.

I float through the coach to the stairs. Dorothea is talking to someone. She sees me and smiles as I descend. Down by the bathrooms and the luggage I push the thing that says *Don't Push* and the door opens, and I stumble out and fall to the ground below.

I get up and start running down the crushed rock toward the back of the train, running from it, running from my mom, burned to ashes in the black box above my seat, running the way I ran when I found her body. I run through the diesel smell with the insects singing in my ears, and when I reach the end of the train I keep running.

I hear a whistle and Dorothea shouting my name. I look over my shoulder and I see her coming after me. She looks very fat when she runs, like her hips get in the way, and I feel bad for making her run, but I can't stop, and I cut to the right down a gravel road, soggy from the flooding, flanked by corn that is higher than my head. There is nothing in my sight except the gravel road that rises gently, and the walls of corn, the sound of their leaves whispering at me to flee, flee, and the sound of my shoes on the road.

After I found my mom dead I ran and ran until a policeman caught me from behind. This time I stop after a minute, because I'm tired and I have nowhere to go, and I miss Dorothea and feel bad about making her chase me. And mostly because now I see corn and corn instead of what I saw in my head that made me start running.

I wait, staring down the road in the direction of my escape, listening to the corn growing.

I think of Dr. Lola. I think of how she touched my hair when she said good-bye on my last day at school in Palm Springs.

I hate remembering that. I hate thinking about it because it makes me feel so strongly about my wish, my stupid fantasy that she was my mother instead of the mom I had. Dr. Lola with her composure, her dry-cleaned clothes, asking me how I'm doing, touching my hair. I hate thinking about it because it'll never be true and because it makes me feel guilty, like I'm betraying the flawed mother I got.

I hear Dorothea's voice calling out to me, but it is Neal's shoes that reach me first. He slows down and stops a couple of steps behind me. I hear him breathing, catching his breath, and I hear my own breath, and the rest of the world holding its breath.

Then his voice. "I wish I could say something that would make you feel better."

I hang my head. I see my sad old shoes. Pink Converse knockoffs.

"You came after me."

"Did you think I wouldn't?"

I don't answer, but I think of what a smile looks like, because I'm glad he did.

"Will you come back with me?" he asks.

"She did the best she could," I say, and a big tear falls onto one of my shoes.

He's quiet for a second, like he's thinking about who I mean. "I'm sure she did, Rydr."

"She was addicted to drugs."

I hear his feet shuffle in the gravel road. "I'm sorry."

"I'm going to leave her here."

He's silent, and with my back to him I picture him looking around at the stalks of corn.

I nod, convincing myself of what I have just said, then turn around and see his handsome face. I hold out my hand to him, and he takes it, and we walk back toward the train together. I feel five years old and a hundred years old. I feel a hundred and five years old.

"You could have caught up to me sooner if you didn't smoke."

"I quit," he says.

"Really? When?"

He looks at his watch. "Fifteen hours and six minutes ago."

I don't say anything. But I feel strangely happy. I feel proud of him.

"And I'm gonna quit Amtrak and commit to my boyfriend."

This makes me stop walking and turn to him. "You are?"

He takes off his hat and runs his fingers front to back though his hair. "It's time. And you're getting off in Chicago." He reaches to my cheek. "Now that I've met you, I can't picture myself working on the train without you on it."

"Wow." That's what I say, but it doesn't really cover what I feel.

Dorothea catches up with us.

"Do you need your puffer?"

"Don't call it a puffer," I say.

Neal clears his throat.

I look to Dorothea. "No, I don't need my inhaler. And—thank you for waking me up to say good-bye to Tenderchunks." I don't know how much I mean it until I say it.

Dorothea frowns. But it isn't a real frown. "Did you have to run out here to tell me that?"

"No, ma'am."

"You done running away?"

"Yes, ma'am."

She gives me a half hug, then raises her walkie-talkie to her mouth. "We're good here. Walking back."

We turn and head down the gravel road together, Neal holding my left hand and Dorothea my right.

I look to Dorothea. "Remember when I told you my father was a movie director in France?"

"Mm-hmm."

"He might be," I say. "But I sincerely doubt it. I've never met him."

"I know, honey."

"He probably died the same way as my mom." I hate this, I hate it so much, but right now I'm hating it quietly and straight on.

It feels good to come clean about that with Dorothea. She starts singing in a voice like she's in church. It's very pretty, something about trails of trouble and paths of victory. I squeeze both of their hands, hers and Neal's, but it won't be long before I have to let go.

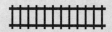

Back on the train, which still isn't moving, I hide out in the bathroom, trying to be invisible. It's one of the bigger bathrooms, and I sit on the little shelf seat instead of out in the coach even though it stinks in there, because it stinks less than being stared at by the other passengers.

Finally I stand and look at the girl in the mirror.

"Where did you think you were going?" she asks.

"I don't know," I say. "Away."

She stares at me, silently ridiculing my lack of a plan. I stare back. It's a stare-down, and I'm the first to break.

"You look older," I say. "When I look at you, I expect you to still be ten years old."

She nods. "Time keeps passing, even if life doesn't go on."

I stare at her for a while. The face looking back at me at times seems hard, at times soft. But I look at her, and I let her look at me.

"So, Dr. Lola . . ."

I can't finish what I start to say. She looks a little annoyed at me for being unable to. Dr. Lola encouraged me to practice telling the girl in the mirror that I love her, and said I should say it until I meant it. But I never did.

"I love you," she says, the girl in the mirror. I see her cherry ChapStick lips move, and I hear the words. I can't say it back, but I think she understands. She looks like she needs to hear it, though. Someday soon I'll say it.

16

WE GET WORD that the Mississippi has subsided enough for the train to be able to leave in an hour.

A deadly sense of finality washes over me. I start biting my nails.

I've been thinking of the box in the overhead luggage rack ever since I got back on the train after running from it.

It's not just a box. It's her ashes. My mother's ashes. I'm going to leave them behind because they're weighing me down with their heaviness. And because she needs to rest.

Saying this is easier than doing it.

I stand up and retrieve my hearts-and-flowers bag. I get the brush and do my hair. I put on cherry Chap-Stick but I can't taste it.

The box is there beside the bag. I take it with both hands and sit down in the aisle seat, holding it on my lap.

It's made of hard black plastic and is heavier than one would think. It's a little bigger than those old-fashioned recipe files, and the same shape. On top beneath clear plastic tape is my mother's full name. *Hanna Hope Hughes.* It has her date of birth and the date of her death, and the name of the mortuary that burned her body.

Dorothea walks up and finds me sitting in her seat on the aisle. I don't look at her, but I can sense her twisting her neck to read the top of the box.

"Oh, honey." She puts her hand on my shoulder. "Is that your momma?"

I nod.

"What a thing to have to carry."

"I wanted to ask you about that," I say. "I was thinking maybe I could spread her ashes. Out here in the fields. So she can rest."

Dorothea is quiet for a moment. I'm sure she's counting in her head how many regulations it would break. Then she raises the walkie-talkie to her mouth.

"Neal. Meet me at your favorite passenger's seat."

In a minute Neal comes through the vestibule into our coach, looking like he fears the worst. Dorothea meets him a couple of aisles away, and they have a quiet word together. Then they come to where I sit and Dorothea speaks.

"Is there anything you'll be needing other than the box?"

I think briefly, then shake my head.

"Okay, honey, let's go."

Dorothea leads the way, with a heaviness in her steps. Neal is right behind me.

We go down the stairs and to the exit from which I escaped not long ago. Dorothea pushes the lever to open the door and drops the yellow step into place. We step out into the day.

Outside has grown warmer. It's quieter, like the insects are being respectful. We stand there for a moment. Then Dorothea says, "You lead the way."

I turn toward the rear of the train, and retrace the steps of my escape, holding the box against me. We walk past the end of the train beside the rail bed, and then take the gravel road into the fields. I had been thinking of the corn, but as we come to higher ground I see a deep green wood ahead.

"Not too far, honey."

"Those woods look nice," I say.

The woods grow more distinct as we draw nearer, dark and peaceful. They aren't any bigger than the Hundred Acre Wood in the Winnie-the-Pooh books my mom read to me when I was very young and she was trying so hard.

At the edge of the field and the beginning of the wood, there's a sign that says *No Hunting*, which makes me glad. Mom was a vegetarian, and raised me the same.

We walk into the shade. I hear a squirrel clamber up a tree.

I count my steps to thirty-four, the age she died at, then fall to my knees in front of an oak tree. Dorothea and Neal halt behind me.

I press the plastic tab and the box pops open. I take the plastic bag from inside and hold it in both hands.

I don't have pliers to open the metal clamp, so I put the top of the bag to my mouth and tear it open with my teeth. I spread the sandy gray remains of my mother on the ground.

Without thinking I put my index finger into my mouth to wet it, and use it to pick up some of the ashes from the ground. Then I lift the bottom of my T-shirt and the scout shirt to put the ashes to my belly button, the place where we had once been connected. I do this like it's a familiar ritual, like I do it every day, like it's something my people have always done, or like I'm doing it for someone else, because I'm not ready to feel it completely.

My hand finds a rock with a jagged edge.

Some people's merit badges are their names on libraries, museums, and universities.

My mother's merit badge is scratched in tear-blurred letters on the trunk of an oak tree, in a small Iowa wood lost to all but squirrels.

"I want you to be proud of me," I say. Only the birds answer. I see her face, framed by pale blond hair. Pretty, melancholy, watching me like I was something beautiful that she couldn't keep. I wait while my eyes water the oak tree.

Finally I stand and turn to Dorothea and Neal. Their eyes are wet, and they search my face as I walk past them. They follow me back silently into the filtered sunlight, down the gravel road past the corn, to the tracks and the yellow step that lifts us back on the train.

17

WE'RE ROLLING AWAY. Rolling toward Chicago, rolling away from my mother.

Dr. Lola suggested that when I was mad or sad about my mom, I should try to remember something positive about her. But every time I searched my memory for something nice, all I could come up with were reasons I was mad at her, and reasons I was sad about her, and reasons I was sorry for myself that she was my mother.

Dr. Lola said I should do the same thing for Gramma, and I came up with the memory of watching her make pancakes. In my mind I'd see her measuring out the ingredients, the flour and sugar and salt and baking soda, and cracking the eggs, and mixing it up and pouring it on the heated skillet.

Even though she had a cigarette dangling from her lips, and subjected me to the smoke, remembering her I focus on the pancakes, their smell, the cold glass of milk, and the butter melting and the syrup flowing over the top of it all. She practically never said anything while she made them or while I ate them. But her making them, and making them the slow way, from scratch, said a lot, I think. She'd look through the window at the morning and smoke her menthols while I ate, but she really felt like my gramma on those mornings.

With my mom I could never come up with anything. Just the scary things and the emergencies and the last stupid words I wrote in my journal.

I won't look in my journal, but sitting in my seat on the train as fields of soybeans roll by, they're shouting at me, the last words. It was so long ago; my penmanship was so young. I won't look in my journal but I can still see the words in my memory. And now I can hear them in my pathetic, naive ten-year-old voice:

Mom is doing so well.

I hate that girl, the stupid ten-year-old who allowed herself to believe that everything could turn out okay, who hoped her mom could stay clean, who let herself be hurt and disappointed again and again.

I bolt from my seat. I hurry down the aisle. By the way people are looking at me, I must look like I'm crazy. I probably am.

I rush down the stairs two at a time, push into the bathroom, and slam the door shut.

The girl in the mirror looks as pissed off at me as I am at her.

"'*Mom is doing so well*,'" she says in a mocking tone. "You're an idiot."

It hurts, but she's just getting started.

"Nobody's ever gonna love you, because you're an idiot. You're a stupid, naive little baby with ugly green hair. Anybody you care about is gonna leave you, and if they can't leave they'll die just to get away from you."

She looks so filled with hate.

"You can't make me cry," I say.

"Right, because you're the password! Mom must have really loved you because she used your name in her email password!"

"Shut up!"

"That's *soooo* special to be the email password for a dead junkie!"

"I hate you!"

"Why don't you just give up like she did?"

My fists fly at her, and I smash at her until she falls

158

in broken pieces onto the counter and into the sink. I kick the toilet, and I kick it again and again until it comes apart, the lid and the seat cracked and scattered. I push on the door but my hands are bleeding, so I kick the door with my heel, and my knockoff sneaker comes apart and the door comes off its hinges. There's a scared-looking old lady standing on the other side, and I move past her up the stairs and limp on one shoe down the aisle to my seat.

I grab my hearts-and-flowers bag and the journal inside, and riffle through it to the page with the words that are hurting me, and blood runs down my arms as I tear the page from the binding. I hobble down the aisle but Dorothea appears in front of me, so I head the other way. The penguin conductor is in that direction, but I rush at him and try to get past, so he grabs hold of my scout shirt and the buttons break, and he holds on to the tail of the shirt and then falls to the floor and hangs on to my leg, and I fall down face-first in the aisle.

Looking at my hands in front of me I see that they really are bleeding a lot. I can hear Dorothea shouting but I don't know what she is saying. I can hear the noise of myself trying to breathe but not being able to.

I feel a strange calm. Pulled to my feet, I allow myself to be given the inhaler. I allow myself to be led into the observation lounge, where the penguin conductor sits with me at a table, blocking my access to the aisle, while Dorothea gets bandages. I allow myself to be a stupid thirteen-year-old who needs all this help.

My breathing quiets, my limbs at rest. In a moment Carlos sits across from me. He has my pink sneaker, and he repairs it with duct tape while Dorothea wraps my hands in gauze. There's blood on my scout shirt and soaking through the bandages, and a bloody handprint on the page torn from my journal.

When he's done fixing my shoe, Carlos picks up the page and examines it. The black ink is visible even through the blood. *Mom is doing so well*. He sets it down and rubs his eyes.

"You can't make me cry," I say. I don't know why I say it.

I haven't seen him look this way before. "If you want to be a poet, you'll have to learn how to cry every now and then."

"What makes you think I want to be a poet?"

He rubs his eyes again with his palms. "You see things others miss." He says it with a weariness, like it's a terrible prognosis. "You've got a light in your eyes."

"That's what . . ."

"Someone else said that already? Probably a poet. It takes one to know one."

"I'm going to buy one of your books when I get a chance," I say. "And I'll write to you to tell you how much I like it."

He doesn't smile. He's looking at my blood-soaked bandages. "Angry at the girl in the mirror?"

It's like he can read my mind. "Yes."

"Why?"

I think a moment. I hadn't really thought about it before. "For . . . I don't know."

"For feeling?"

I nod.

"For holding hope in her heart?"

I nod again.

Carlos folds and unfolds his hands. "The best kind of people are people who feel, and who hold hope in their hearts. Even if it sometimes means being hurt and disappointed. Even if it *always* means being hurt and disappointed."

I look away, and then down to Dorothea's hands finishing up on mine.

"You stay here with Carlos while I find an incident report," she says, getting to her feet. "Somehow I've run out of them." First she hands me my hearts-and-flowers bag. "So you won't have any excuse to leave Carlos and try to run off again."

She walks away.

Carlos examines the bag. "You don't strike me as the hearts-and-flowers sort."

I reach inside it for my cherry ChapStick. It's hard to take the cap off with my hands hurt and bandaged, and the pain is starting to get to me now that my anger is gone. I spread the cherry on my lips and offer it to him.

He smiles a tiny smile. "No thanks."

I put it back.

"On second thought, I'll have some. Add it to my list of life experiences."

I give it to him. He takes the cap off, smells it, raises his eyebrows. "You don't have leprosy or anything else I should know about?"

"Leprosy?"

"Never mind." He spreads it on. "Tasty." He licks his lips. "I don't know how you can put this stuff down."

"I can't."

He adjusts his collar. He's worn a different shirt every day. "So, Rydr, to this point you've managed to avoid revealing where you're going. And practically everything else about yourself, for that matter."

"I've got an air of mystery to me, don't I?"

He smiles, shakes his head, and takes a sip of his coffee.

"What about you?" I ask. "All I know about you

is that you have kids that are grown, you like cross-words, and you change clothes every day somehow."

"That's pretty much me in a nutshell."

"No, *really*. Where do you change clothes?"

"They gave me a sleeper, so I get to travel in luxury. But I prefer the company of the masses such as yourself."

"Who do you mean, *they*?"

"Amtrak. I'm getting a stipend and a free sleeper room to ride the train and write poems about it."

"Really? Wow."

"It's pretty cool. That's about as richly rewarded as poets ever are. I mean, there's a reason I know how to repair shoes with duct tape."

He pushes my shoe across the table. I admire his duct-tape handiwork and then slip it on.

"Speaking of poets." I reach into my bag and pull out *Howl*. "Have you heard of this guy?"

Carlos takes it. "Heck yeah. It's probably my favorite volume ever." He flips through it, then stops at the front and studies it carefully. His eyes meet mine. "Holy cow. How did you get a signed copy? Is this legit?"

"Huh?"

He shows me the title page, with two signatures in black ink.

"That's Ginsberg's signature, and that one is

Ferlinghetti's. He's the publisher, and a poet himself. A great poet. And you have both?"

"Is that unusual?"

Carlos just stares at me.

I think of the expression on Tenderchunks's face when I told him I was keeping *Howl*. A chill runs down my spine. "Tenderchunks gave it to me."

"Tenderchunks?"

I tug at the lapel of my scout shirt to communicate it to Carlos.

"Wow. His shirt and a signed copy of *Howl*."

"He said it would change my life. And I feel like it has. I feel like it was written just for me."

Carlos tilts his head a little as he regards me. "Yep. It took more than fifty years, and it probably had to change hands a few times. But I think it finally found the girl it was written for."

It's at this moment that I know for sure that I'm going to be a poet. As soon as my hands heal I'm going to write poems, and the first one will begin with the last words I wrote in my journal. *Mom is doing so well.*

"I hope Tenderchunks at least got a kiss out of it," Carlos says. He searches my expression.

I don't answer, and I try not to smile. Carlos smiles for me. Then Dorothea sits at my side, putting a paper form in front of me.

"All right, honey. I'm getting writer's cramp filling out these dang incident reports. Let's make this the last one, okay?"

After the forms I ask Dorothea if I can go downstairs to see Neal.

"First we need to talk about what happens when you get to Chicago." She unfolds a sheet of paper.

"Do I have a choice?"

She doesn't answer. Instead she reads from the paper with a lilt in her voice, like she's describing the amenities at someplace fun, like I really was going to Disneyland all along.

"'Accompany subject and her luggage as she disembarks train at Union Station in Chicago. On the platform you will be met by Officer Barney or other representative who will present credentials and sign for her, after which point subject will no longer be in your custody.'"

I turn to look out the window. Fields are giving way to suburbs. Chicago is drawing near.

"'Officer Barney will then transport subject to Cook County Social Services. Prior to being introduced to relative who will henceforth serve as custodian, subject will be oriented and screened for parasitic infestation.'"

Carlos clears his throat.

"I don't have lice," I say.

"Maybe I shouldn't be reading it aloud." Dorothea folds the paper and puts it away. "I'm sure everything will be just fine when we get to Chicago." She pats me on top of my hand, then gets up from the table and walks down the aisle.

I'm left with Carlos. I turn from the window to his face.

"He can only count to seven on his fingers."

"Who?" Carlos asks.

"My great-uncle. Apparently he's missing one finger from one hand and two from the other."

One side of his mouth turns up in a smile.

"That's all I know about him. That, and his monthly check will get bigger when I'm living with him."

Carlos watches me. He's like Dr. Lola, and Neal, just waiting for what I'll say next.

"It's like our branch of the family tree is diseased. It's dead and dying and at the very end is one little leaf that's still green. Or one small, unripe fruit that doesn't yet know the branch is dead. But that little leaf is about to be carried away by the wind." I bite a fingernail. "Or that little fruit is about to fall to the ground. And now it knows it."

Carlos shifts in his seat. He folds his hands on the table before him, and leans toward me. "What will the little leaf do when it's cast to the wind?"

I shrug. "It'll try to fly."

"And what will the little fruit do if it falls to earth?"

It's almost unbearably nice for him to wonder, to ask. "It'll hit the ground running."

"Those are very good answers." His eyes look melty, the way that mine feel. "I think you need a merit badge on that scout shirt."

I look down at the area above the pocket. Loose threads mark where the badges had been. "Tenderchunks ripped his badges off."

"Probably because of who awarded them." Carlos opens his journal and begins working at it with his pencil. "But I hope you'll want to keep this one."

I lean forward to observe him drawing a small square. Then he hides what he's drawing with his other hand.

"No peeking." He folds the paper and tears it until it's like a little badge. He backs it with the duct tape he repaired my shoes with, and hands it to me. "I hereby bestow upon you the highest honor I am aware of."

I look at it in my palm. It has a drawing of an old-fashioned pen and the word *poet*. "Me?"

He nods. "No question about it."

"I haven't even written one yet."

He looks at me patiently. "Maybe not on paper."

I stick it to my shirt, above the pocket where Tenderchunks's badges had been. "But I will," I say.

"I know you will." He stands. He slides *Howl* across the table to me. "Try not to bleed on this." Then he shakes his head. "I don't know. Maybe you *should* bleed on it. Make it even more valuable." He smiles, then takes the duct tape and his journal and leaves the table.

I watch him go, then I look down at my new badge. I feel like a poet already.

Outside the window Illinois rushes past too quickly, so I head downstairs to the snack bar. I approach the counter.

"Time for one more snack?" Neal asks.

"I would love a snack, but to be completely honest, I've been broke since the Japanese convenience store at Union Station in Los Angeles. And every time I try to make some money, Dorothea makes me give it back. So I'm broke, and I'm really hungry, and yes, I'd love a snack. You've been very generous, but you probably didn't know how desperate and dependent on you and Carlos I have been. So I am here to come clean about that." I clear my throat, which was tightening up as I spoke. "I'm starving."

Neal looks shocked. "I had no idea. I mean, I kind of had an idea, but I had no idea that you'd be—"

"It's my fault," I say. "I should have said something. I should have just told you I didn't have anything to eat."

He shakes his head. "Please, take whatever you'd like. Eat until you're full. And I'm so sorry. I should have known. I shouldn't have made you come around waiting for me to figure it out."

I love this man. I love all humankind at this moment. I take an orange, and a veggie burger, and an apple.

"Also, every time I called you Nate or Nick or whatever I was only pretending to not know what your name was. I was afraid that if you knew I remembered your name you'd somehow figure out that I've had this silly fantasy where you're my dad. But since that's never going to happen, I guess I'm okay with you knowing."

"Wow. I don't know what to say."

"And when I won the money and I had to give it back, Tenderchunks gave it to me again. So I could have given it to you then but instead I used it to buy this bracelet from a little girl at the station in La Junta." I hold up my arm to display it.

"That's very cute."

"I want you to have it. Because I should have given you the money."

"It wasn't my money. It's Amtrak's."

"But I can't give it to Amtrak. Amtrak doesn't want this bracelet."

Neal smiles, but he looks like he'll cry. "But I do. Thank you, R-Y-D-R."

I untie it and he holds out his arm in offering. His wrist is perfect but the bracelet is a little snug.

"These colors," he says. "This'll remind me of the landscape we traveled through while you changed my life."

"What do you mean?"

Neal sits on the stool. "The way you were disappointed in me for smoking, and worried. It made me think about how hard it must be for my boyfriend."

"Chuck."

"Right. Chuck. And *you* just met me, but he and I have been together for years."

I nod. I'm thinking of my mom.

"With what you've been through, how you must have worried about your mom, wishing she could stop . . ." He read my mind. He wipes his eyes against his sleeve. "I have a home, with someone I love and who loves me waiting there. You taught me how lucky I am."

I feel pressure behind my eyes. "I didn't mean to teach you anything."

"One day you'll have that too. A home, where

someone who loves you is waiting." He puts his hand on mine. "I hope it's soon."

I had it for three days, here on the train. I smile weakly.

Then Neal takes off his conductor's cap and puts it on my head.

"In case it rains," he says.

18

EATING FOOD IS a good way to distract your-self from unhappy feelings. When I finish the food I got from Neal, the view through the windows in the observation lounge gets sadder. This is especially true after Naperville, the last stop before the end of the line.

It's all ending, always ending. It's ending again.

So I leave the observation lounge. I smile at Carlos like I'm going to see him again in just a minute and there'll be another chance to say a real good-bye later. But there probably won't be.

I always cry at endings. Except I don't cry. So I cut out before the endings if I can. Carlos will get off from the sleeper cars and get lost in the crowd, and I'll be taken away by another guy wearing beige, another Smokey Bear hat.

I sit moping in my seat as the suburbs of Chicago roll by my window. A freight train passes in the opposite direction, half a mile of tanker cars and flat cars and boxcars boxcars boxcars.

Dorothea appears, standing in the aisle, holding her hand out to me. She looks tired. It's been a long trip, and I haven't made it easy on her.

"Come on, Honey."

I look away. But I scoot over to the aisle and stand up. I follow her as she says something into her walkie-talkie. I feel like I'm in trouble. Like all of my misdeeds on the train are finally catching up to me.

We go through the vestibule into the lounge car, and stop at the top of the stairs.

"Neeeeal!" she shouts down the stairs, then we keep on walking through another vestibule into the dining car with its fancy white tablecloths, the table where I sat with Tenderchunks. Then into and through the sleeper cars, one and then another. Neal appears behind me. I turn and he smiles.

We go down the stairs and stand by one of the bathrooms at the exit. Looking out the window, I can see we're slowing down. I can feel it.

"Am I getting thrown off the train?" I ask.

Dorothea doubles over laughing.

Neal puts his hand on my shoulder. "If anyone asks,

this never happened," he says.

Dorothea slaps him on the back. "Oh, this'd be the icing on the cake."

Neal reaches into his vest pocket. "We have something for you. Inspired by Carlos."

"We gotta be quick." Dorothea takes something from her back pocket. "Neal thought I should say 'resourceful' but that's a lot of letters for a small badge."

It's a button as big as a silver dollar that's been covered with masking tape, on which she has drawn a lightbulb and the word *crafty*.

She pins it to my inherited scout shirt. "The lightbulb is supposed to mean that you're full of clever ideas."

"I'm glad it doesn't say 'trouble.'" I don't want to cry. I never cry.

Dorothea puts her hand on my shoulder. "Honey, I'm not saying you were any trouble, but if you were, you're worth it."

"Thank you for letting me spread my mother's ashes. For everything."

She gives me a full hug this time, and I hug her back.

"I had a hard time choosing just one merit," Neal says. "So I chose the one that I think will serve you best." His hands tremble as he pins it to me. "It's gotten you this far."

I look down at the button. It has the word *strong*

written inside a drawing of a heart.

"I don't know what to say." I really don't. I picture the girl in the mirror with the green hair, and I wonder if she really is these things they're saying. I hope she is.

The train stops.

I look out the window. The sky is gray. We're alongside an old brick factory with broken windows. Dorothea opens the door and the smell of a city in summer comes in, a smell I remember from long ago, different than the smell of Palm Springs, where it's almost always summer. Neal jumps out onto the broken gray rock of the rail bed, and reaches up to me.

"Come on! Hurry!"

I hold his hand and jump to his arms. He sets me down, then pulls me along, running toward the front of the train. We run past the engines and to a hatch at the front of the locomotive. The engineer's annoyed face softens when he sees me.

Neal pushes me up the steps and I'm inside the locomotive, standing at the controls. He's right behind me, and the engineer shuts the hatch and hurries to his seat.

I look out the big window as the engineer moves a couple of levers. The train starts moving again. He gestures to the seat next to him. I look to Neal and he smiles and nods. I sit.

We roll forward, and I take it all in through the big

windshield—the view coming to me instead of passing by.

Everything gets larger. I can see where I'm going. I feel Neal's hands on my shoulders, and I melt into the chair.

"What's your name, girl?"

"Rydr," I hear myself say.

We pick up speed.

"Neal tells me you're more than a little sad. And maybe just a bit scared."

I nod.

"Well, I'm very sorry to hear that. I can't promise that it'll make anything better, but why don't you give a little push on that big orange button to your left?"

I look up at Neal, and he nods. I reach for it, and give it a cautious tap. An enormous horn hiccups.

The engineer smiles. "Don't be shy, now."

I give it a firmer push, and hold it for a second. It's me making that big noise.

"That's better," the engineer says.

Neal opens the side windows, and the noise of the train gets bigger, bouncing back from the city, and the sound of the world rushing by.

The gray blanket that has been the sky for three days moves aside, like we've reached land's end and seen the sea of blue. The skyscrapers of Chicago loom in the distance, basking in the evening sun that has just appeared.

The new life that has been forced upon me awaits. Tears stream down my face.

"Do it again," Neal says. "Make it cry. Make it *howl.*"

I push down on the horn, and hold it.

I laugh.

I push the horn in short bursts. It is the spray can that paints the bright graffiti on the brick walls beside the tracks.

I hold it down until the most seasoned pigeons fly from me in fear.

I lean on the horn, and the pedestrians at crosswalks three blocks away cover their ears.

I blast the horn and the agencies shudder, the sick clinics tremble, the asylum doors are blown from their hinges.

I smash down on the horn and I howl, I cry, I shout every cuss word I know, and possibly some I'm making up.

I scream for my mother and at my mother, *you left me, you left me,* and I curse the father who wasn't a dad, everyone who abandoned me and died on me, and I hear myself shouting *Moloch!* again and again, beneath the wailing of the horn, until it's all out of me, the madness, for the moment at least, and I'm spent.

My eyes are fresh from tears. I take a deep breath and reach up to the hands on my shoulders. Neal's hands, which have been there all along.

I watch Chicago coming to me.

The tall buildings grow taller until they loom above, towering.

It is Moloch,
This city I am being fed to,
The buildings of brick and steel,
Blind windows filled with strangers.

It comes to me as I watch it coming.
Through the windshield
Of the locomotive
It comes to me

It is upon me

It glows
In the radiance
Of my eyes

ACKNOWLEDGMENTS

Thanks as always to the mighty Central Phoenix Writer's Workshop, and especially first readers Kelsey Pinckney and Michelle Edwards.

Thanks to Jake Friedman, for not letting me quit.

To the Muse for knowing my address, and for bringing me Rydr and her story.

To Elvis Presley and Allen Ginsberg, for their voices.

To my wonderful agent, Wendy Schmalz, for being the one who said *yes*.

To Rosemary Brosnan at HarperCollins, for the green light.

To my editor, Karen Chaplin, for helping make this story as good as it could be.

And to anyone currently sitting on a train, or anywhere else, reading a novel or poem.

TURN THE PAGE FOR
A SNEAK PEEK AT THE
NEXT NOVEL FROM
PAUL MOSIER

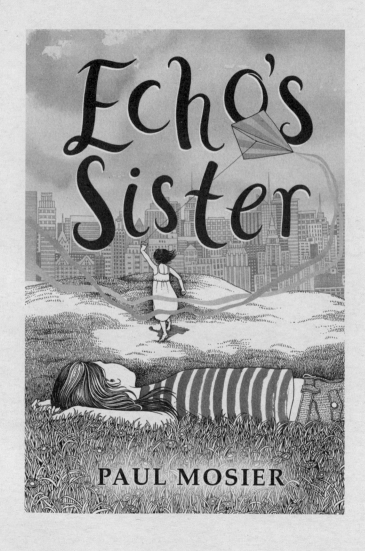

Echo's
Sister

PAUL MOSIER

1

TODAY IS THE first day of school, and it's gonna be fantastic.

I think this as I sit on the toilet in the second-floor bathroom of the Village Arts Academy in New York City, looking at a page in my tiny journal with a list of things to say to all my new classmates. The carefully crafted phrases on my list are sure to make me a big hit with all these new kids.

Technically the kids aren't new. They're just new to me. I've been going to public school my whole life, but now I'm starting seventh grade at this private arts academy.

I'll make all kinds of new friends as long as I stick to the list of things to say and don't allow conversation to stray into dangerous subjects, like money. The kids at this school generally have much more money than my family does. We can barely afford to live here in Manhattan, even though my mom is a semi-famous dress designer. The other kids mostly have rich parents who work on Wall Street. They probably all get dropped off in limousines, while our plan is for Dad to walk me to school every day.

I'm not sure why everything is so expensive in the city, because the apartments are tiny and falling apart. Or at least ours is. My dad says that the correct term for expensive and tiny and falling apart is *charming*. Mom seems to agree with him. I guess our neighborhood, which is called Greenwich Village, is kind of pretty with its trees in the sidewalk planters. Before Mom and Dad had me and Echo—my little sister—it probably felt much roomier. Now there's four of us crammed into an apartment we can barely afford and that we can't afford to leave.

Seventh grade is obviously the luckiest grade, so I'm sure that the Village Arts Academy won't crumble to the ground, even though it's, like, 150 years old. At least not while I'm in seventh grade, the luckiest. And there's really nothing wrong with this school that a million dollars' worth of disinfectant couldn't fix. Particularly in the bathrooms. This is foremost in my thoughts as I sit on the toilet reviewing my list of things to say to make a good impression on my new classmates.

In addition to Don't mention money in any way, my list says Don't compliment anyone's clothes. Everyone here wears the same uniform, so obviously that would sound stupid. And if I complimented another girl's clothes that would also be complimenting my *own* clothes, which would make me sound conceited.

My list also says Don't ask where the bathroom is. That'll be perfectly easy to not do as I'm already here. I just need to remember how to get back once I leave. Sitting in the stall is a good place to collect one's thoughts and gather one's courage, as long as nobody thinks I spend too much time in here, like there's something wrong with me or something.

It's not that I'm embarrassed that I'm, like, a physical human being who has to use the bathroom. It's just that in books and cartoons and movies the characters never have to pee. So it seems weird to bring it to anyone's attention.

One of the most important items on the list is Don't introduce yourself as Laughter, which is the actual name my parents gave me. Instead I go by "El," as in the sound of the letter my name begins with. When other girls hear it they'll just think my name is Elle, which immediately makes me sound like I've stepped from the pages of a fashion magazine, even if I'm wearing exactly the same thing as every other girl in school.

But maybe it isn't good to sound like I've stepped from the pages of a fashion magazine? I turn back to an earlier entry in my tiny journal and add it to my list of things to wonder about.

Seeing Laughter on the list reminds me that I need to tell my first-period teacher that I go by my nickname before he does the roll call. I only have about three minutes before the bell rings so I flush the toilet even though I didn't pee, so the other girls in the bathroom won't think I was just hanging out in the stall like it's a magical unicorn vortex.

Before closing my tiny journal I notice that everything listed is things *not* to say, except Hello!

That's easy enough to remember.

Hello!

I strike the exclamation point with my pencil so I don't sound too eager.

Hello.

It occurs to me I've just said "Hello" out loud twice while looking at the list, so I now must pretend to be having a telephone conversation in the stall so that the other girls in the restroom don't think I'm someone who sits on the toilet saying hello

4

to herself, which apparently I am.

"Yeah, I'm at school, just getting ready for first hour. Uh-huh. Yeah. Okay. Really? No way! Yep. All right. Smashing. That'd be delightful. Okay. *Ciao!*"

I might have overdone it with my conversation, which is all kinds of make-believe. In my mind I was pretending to have a conversation with Maisy, my best friend from my old school and my whole life, but I haven't actually spoken to her in weeks because she was in France for most of the summer.

Also I want Maisy to think that everything is going to be great with me at my new school, and I've had a hard time feeling like I could sound convincing. I've been really worried that I won't make any friends, and I'm sure Maisy will be able to tell I'm worried if she hears my voice. My parents won't even let me take my cell phone to school because they think I'm famous for losing things.

Finally I close my tiny journal and tuck it away in my shirt pocket, then wait a half minute to give everyone in the bathroom a chance to forget what they've just heard. I stand, straighten my uniform skirt and button-up shirt, put my book bag over my shoulder, slide the lock in the stall door, and exit with an air of nonchalance.

I avoid eye contact with the six or seven other girls

5

chatting in front of the mirror as I wash my hands at the sink. I glance at my face in the mirror, my light brown hair and green eyes, then wipe the chocolate from the corner of my mouth 'cause it won't do to have everyone jealous that I had a chocolate doughnut for breakfast.

Then I hurry down the hall, keeping my feet close to the wooden floors so I won't sound like I'm running, though I practically am. Then inside room 211 and to the front of the class, where there's a really good-looking man standing. But I don't care that he's gorgeous because boys don't have any effect on me.

"Hello," he says.

"Hello," I say. He's got wavy dark hair and a smiley smile. He has patches on the elbows of his sport coat.

"Are you in my first-hour class?"

"Yes," I begin, then take my voice down a few notches. "And I wanted to alert you to a mistake with my name."

"Oh? What mistake is that?" He tilts his head.

I lean in closer. "The record says my name is Laughter, but it's actually El."

"Laughter?" he asks way too loudly.

I wince. "Please just call me El when you take attendance."

He smiles. "How about I just laugh and you can

6

wave at me from your desk?"

I try not to smile, because he needs to know how serious I am about this.

"All right, Miss El," he says. "Please take your seat, it's almost time for—"

The bell rings long and loud, interrupting him. He smiles, and I smile back, not because he's good-looking and charming but because it's what you do when someone smiles at you.

When I turn around every desk is taken except for one in the front row, which is exactly where I was hoping not to sit. It would be one thing if the last open seat was in the front row but nearest the door, but it's right in the center, like I'm the hood ornament of the class.

"That one isn't taken." It's a girl, smiling and pointing at the seat to her right. The hood ornament seat. I furrow my brow. I'm not sure whether she's smiling because she's nice or because she's mean and fully aware that it's the very worst seat in class.

I sit in the chair, which is connected to the wooden desk, and sink down as low as I can without drawing attention to myself.

Teacher-man turns his back to the class and begins writing on the blackboard, which may possibly be as old as this building. The chalk taps and squeaks.

Then he turns to the class and smiles. I see the name he has written on the board and my jaw drops. There's a low murmur from the class behind me.

"Good morning, class, and welcome to seventh-grade English. My name is Mr. Dewfuss, an unfortunate gift from my ancestors, who made lives for themselves finding things to eat in the swamps of central Europe. Generally the enunciation of my name is followed by a chorus of . . ." He pauses and glances beneath raised eyebrows directly at me. "*Laughter.* So instead I'd prefer it if you called me Mr. D."

He returns to the chalkboard and erases everything in his name except the letter *D.*

I sit up straight. This is definitely gonna be the best year ever, and—worst seat or not—seventh-grade English with Mr. D is gonna be my favorite class.

The rest of English class is pretty much perfect. We're beginning with a unit on Emily Dickinson, who is maybe my favorite poet ever. Her poems are surprising, even when you've read them a million times. But I don't let anyone in class know I've already read them a million times, 'cause I'm not sure if my classmates realize how cool it is that I have.

The bell rings, the class rises with the sounds of backpacks zipping and chairs and desks dragging on the wood floors. Having been totally absorbed in the discussion, I am the last to pack my backpack, the last to leave the class. I smile at Mr. D and he smiles back as I leave the room and enter the rest of the school day.

I glide down the hall past trophy cases, which don't have figures of athletes because they don't really do sports much at this school. So if I'm gonna keep winning tennis trophies it's gonna have to be at the racquet club, where Mom and Dad signed me up at the beginning of summer. Instead this school has cases with black-and-white photographs of bow-tied teachers standing beside children of earlier generations who won academic decathlons and art scholarships, and trophies that have no balls or bats or racquets at all.

I catch a glimpse of an old photo showing my high-school-aged dad standing before a giant canvas with a big paintbrush in hand, looking smug, but I don't stop to examine it. I pretend not to notice a photo of my pretty teenage mom smiling beside a dress form featuring one of her early designs from high school. I pretend not to notice these things because I don't want to draw attention to the fact my parents went to school here, which might make it obvious they can only afford to send me here because of the discount given to legacy students. I've already seen the photos anyway, when I took the tour early in the summer, so I keep my nose pointed down the hall in the direction of my next class.

The rest of the day is almost perfect. Math is, like, a whole year behind what I was doing at public school last year, so I'll be able to skate through it.

In history class we talk about the Minoan civilization, where kids our age had to survive jumping over a bull's horns as a rite of passage. I think the teacher, Mr. Grimm, wants us to feel like we have it easy since we don't have to jump over a bull's horns to get a passing grade, and I'm pretty sure he's going to try to make it as hard as possible for us. But I sit next to a nice girl named Emy, who invites me to sit with her at café fourth hour.

Mom packed the best-ever lunch: an almond butter and blackberry jelly sandwich, tahini coleslaw, and mango slices. I eat it with Emy in the basement cafeteria, which has tall windows through which you can watch the people walking by on the sidewalk. I share my mango with Emy and remember not to stray from my list of safe topics for conversation. I can expand that list after she and I have become inseparable. And when I get home I'll call Maisy and tell her how wonderful everything is turning out to be, and how I made a great new friend, but not to worry, as Emy will never take the place of her.

In physical education I score a goal in street hockey, which we play outside on the actual tree-lined street while bright orange barricades at either end keep cars away.

In science, a dark-haired boy who would be considered cute—by girls who care about that sort of thing—keeps looking at me, which is a good thing only because it's better than *not* attracting the notice of any of them. I mean, boys can't really help themselves at this age, and being noticed by one of them means that there's probably nothing terribly wrong with me physically.

Unless of course he's looking at me because there *is* something terribly wrong with me physically. I pull out my tiny journal and find the list of things to wonder about, and add that to it. But I'm pretty sure he's looking at me because I activated his girl-crazy radar. Boys can be so clueless they often fail to notice serious imperfections. Like one ear being way higher than the other.

I guess that's kinda sweet of them.

One ear being way higher than the other is actually one of several items on the list of serious imperfections from which I suffer. This list is also found in my tiny journal, but I try not to spend too much time looking at it. It's bad for my morale.

Seventh hour is art, and the teacher is a woman named Miss Numero Uno, who actually knows my dad from way back when he painted a lot. Miss Numero Uno doesn't embarrass me too much by drawing attention to her knowing my dad. This is fortunate because she is potentially quite embarrassing, the way that artists sometimes are. She has tattoos all over her arms and black hair with frighteningly sharp bangs, and today wears jeans with paint splattered all over them so everyone will know she's legit. She has a way of looking at you like she's deciding whether you'd be a good subject to paint, which takes a little getting used to.

Also, Miss Numero Uno isn't an actual name. I'm pretty sure that's, like, an Art World name. Her real name is probably Betty Johnson or something like that. But obviously I'm completely okay with it if she wants to be called something other than the name she was given. I totally get it.

Miss Numero Uno has us do something she calls "free expression on newsprint" while she stares out the windows of the fourth floor, which is the top level of the Village Arts Academy. I draw her staring out the windows, and as I look from Miss Numero Uno to my paper and back she strikes a pose. Her profile is backlit, like the emperor Napoleon tasting victory in the painting on the cover of our history book from third hour. She just stands there holding the pose like it's perfectly normal, even though I'm the only one drawing her and everyone else seems to be avoiding looking at her. I draw her in deep gray charcoal, and it looks pretty good.

But I start to regret my choice of subject when it occurs to me that we will be turning in the newsprint for her to evaluate. Maybe she never knew how ridiculous she looks posing against the window, in which case it's probably not good to be the one to bring it to her attention. When I'm done I give the drawing a goofy smile to disguise the drama of the pose, and so she won't think I'm very good. I don't want to draw attention to myself as particularly talented, either.

When the final bell rings I already have my book bag packed and ready to go. I leave my newsprint on my table as instructed and drift out of the art room, out of the smells of clay and linseed-oil paint, and into the hall.

I feel dreamy. It's been the best first day of school ever, and it's gonna be an amazing year.

I scan the throng of students moving down the hall, down the wide stairs, down the main hall toward the front doors, but I don't see Emy. Nor do I see the boy who stared at me in science class. But I'll see them again tomorrow. Because this school is now *my* school, and these will be my classmates and friends, more and more each day.

Out the doors I go, into the warm September afternoon. Down the wide gray steps, onto the sidewalk.

My dad is standing there.

I stop cold.

"Why are you here?"

He smiles awkwardly, bounces on his heels. "Just wanted to see how your first day went."

I frown. This is not part of the plan. He wasn't supposed to meet me. I was supposed to walk home myself.

"What's wrong?" I ask.

My classmates stream past. A terrible feeling descends upon me, like the sky is falling.

"What?" I ask.

"Come on." His arms reach out to me, ready for an embrace.